Fresh Linen is Best Served Cold

Steve Jones

Published by New Generation Publishing in 2022

Copyright © Steve Jones 2021

First Edition

The author asserts the moral right under the Copyright, Designs and Patents Act 1988 to be identified as the author of this work.

All Rights reserved. No part of this publication may be reproduced, stored in a retrieval system or transmitted, in any form or by any means without the prior consent of the author, nor be otherwise circulated in any form of binding or cover other than that which it is published and without a similar condition being imposed on the subsequent purchaser.

This is a work of fiction. Any resemblance to actual events or locales or persons, living or dead, is entirely coincidental.

ISBN   978-1-80369-029-2

www.newgeneration-publishing.com

New Generation Publishing

There's something sexy, attractive about those who play a musical instrument. Music and Mathematics are true universal language disciplines of the human race. These two masters are instrumental in exciting the mortality and spiritual experience of the individual.

My wife and I have followed "live music" for many years.

We have sorely missed you guys.

I dedicate this small book to all those musicians who had their jack plugs pulled as a consequence of the Covid 19 Epidemic.

Thank you, all the boys and girls of the NHS who grew old and tired during their Covid shifts.

This Book

This book is the product of too much time on my hands during Covid19.

There are many others out there, all writing for the same reason, to leave something behind. I have sent this book to the publisher rather impatiently. At the time of writing, I am a CEV (Clinically Extremely Vulnerable). The date I type this is 26/01/2021, is the day it transpires that a vaccine is being held up for political reasons - there's a whole story here, but it will be written by a professional someday. In the meantime, I am an ordinary working class guy who is concerned for his family and my own psychological health. I have written quite a lot of stuff, - 5 books in all over the years, this one is a soul searching, if not a self-indulgent contribution eked out of fear and uncertainty.

Other books by the author:-

The Edge of Feedback - Semi Autobiographical Fun.
Out Rage – Short Stories, a play and some poems.
Shades of Blue – Soul Searching Prose Poetry.
Kanita's Story* - 269 page parked up novel
Through a Glass Darkly* – Adventures of two time traveling spirits.

* These books have been *printed* for posterity at the moment.

When I buy books to study and educate myself I always scribble notes in them. This edition has blank pages for you to criticise my work and write your own stuff on the train!

Steve Jones.

Old Boys Lament

Of course I'm like a spoiled child,
Having spent over sixty seven years fairly wild.
I did as I liked, so they say,
I played and prayed and did it –my way,
Excuse the cliché

Now I see straight,
No need to wait.
Must really take the bait,
And submit to defeat.
My spirit has left my feet,
As dead as nails I can no longer reach.

I shall soon be hauled from this existence,
Sorry Love!
I can no longer do the distance
I leave you now these final words;

I look at your arse,
And I see it rotating,
While my old heart gently bleats.

Explosion or Implosion

If Explosives are treated right they become Unstable.

Depressed,
Dejected, so blue am I.
Underfoot there is soggy cold soil.
Above a tear saturated sky.
The sun is an exploding match,
At the end of my cigarette.
The moon, a child's bedroom night light,
Flickering atop of an amazon peninsular.
Alone, basking, so insular.

A trip to the letter box-nothing.
Social media isn't feeding ya
You should have taken heed,
Essential trips only.

Compression is winning,
Anxiety, paranoia,
Is just something else to annoy ya.

Try to get things into my head,
Running over the things I should have fucking said,
And God forbid, I never did, please help me escape this pain
Crack this coconut, I want to be a slut of life again.

Let's Burst Together

Press me, undress me,
Like you do with your garlic clove.
Drop me in olive oil and cider vinegar,
Add some herbs and spices too.
The longer I last in there,
The more pleasure coming to you.
After this we shall share seed and pips,
Which have peppered your lips.
In a passionate kiss so bruising,
And show, it might,
A sensually obtained,
All becoming love bite.

Oh my love!
You are so Ricotta stuffed pepper.
I use my fingers to pull you out,
I savour your oily preservative,
Compress your red.
With my tongue tease out the cheese
Swallow it whole drowning
And listen through your tummy
At your body orchestra moaning.

Possibilities & Restrictions

2020

I was welcomed into this day by a tube of toothpaste. Under pressure it gave me what I wanted, the right amount, colour, taste, texture, blue streaks, minty smell and above all whilst it performed its birth it remained silent-giving me pleasure; a sensation without complication, corruption free!

The distance between my naked body and the canal is 10.015 meters (15mm of frosted glass). My eyes are frosted too.

My humble abode is 53 years old. I am 67 years old. Canal history outside of our demise but only by 1.7 meters is silent. Silent as in what is done, is done. The width of this particular stretch of canal within eyesight before bends used to be in parenthesis via industry. Now the vista is all shrubs, trees, nests of birds and the roofs of houses. The muddy water following a storm is a lilied stage for the performance of coots, herons, moorhens, swans, ducks and dark fish.

All I visualise through this damn misted bathroom window is an idyllic vision merging into the past. In reality I know that there are rotten corpses of working class men and women floating there, holding hands, viciously dead.

The dead are the forgotten slaves of industry. Thick water tidies up the past. Narrowboats blend cadavers with propellers and a wag of rudder. The past and all the suffering of mankind drowned in ignorance.

I dress. Sartorial consideration has tiptoed away. I am not an individual I am, in all entirety, a part of this diseased and corrupt enigma of engineered virus and conspiracy. My Intellect has been dumbed down. I stand in queues with all the humility of Oliver Twist. At a Nano second I can be rendered destitute.

My hair is long; my teeth, yellow and black leaves of autumn willow. I shop to live. This is 2020, a year that is levelling the human inspiration and rolling individuality into the canal. I open the kitchen door to a damp cool breeze and visit the watery grave. I squat and flick crumbs of unpalatable bread into the beaks of ducks.

My eyes drift. I hear a gentle plink of water. Between the Hawthorne bushes some way to my right and on the opposite side of the canal, I spy the tip of a fishing rod.

This is exactly what I don't want. At this time I do not want the company of someone content. I long for someone who is lost; lost in a cascade of sparks and flames. Above all this person has to be female, a companion.

I walk left down the canal tow path. I look back, the rod has been successful, I turn, and walk back silently. Discs of ripples transmit themselves as a rod tip bends. Out comes a ragged fish flapping like a wet flannel. I feel I need to see what has caught this fish. Like a sapper I inch forward, my eyes sharp and keen. There appears to be a clear archway through the shrubbery where the rod and fish have fled. There's no evidence of a landing net. A blast of channelled breeze opens up a cathedral door of forestry and I see her. My heart misses a beat, pacemaker thuds, I catch my breath.

I know; oh Lord, she has the face and figure of my imaginary fierce companion.

All at once my mood, so dark, has lifted with exaltation. She is young and petite as a crocus. I stand proud, upright and visible. She pretends I am not here. Her angelic figure crouches down and her nimble fingers extract a hook. Her clothes are not what I would expect for a fishing session. From nowhere a young child, calls out and appears at her feet. The young woman starts to tidy up the detritus of an improvised angling session, her hand reaches out and the child grips and they are gone.

I feel so ashamed. I shouldn't be having these feelings and longings. My beloved was taken in the first wave of the virus. I waved to her and she never waved back.

With this thought I retreat indoors. There will be "how are you?" calls shortly from *our* estranged children. If I were to answer "fucking suicidal, mourning, and lonely!" what then? So like a struggling government, the use of lies and deception are acceptable in this instance. No one person is all hours wise. The children will guess at the lie, and have no choice but to accept it. There are too many mysteries, twice as many possibilities, hardly any luck, and this simply means from birth it's a complete minefield of human to human manipulation so one can be taller than the other.

This is my first entry. They told me to write down stuff as and when. I cannot think of anything. I miss him. I don't miss him beating me. I cannot get over the way he changed. I always kept myself tidy. It was after I gave birth to Sappho. He spent more time up the pub, he is a flirt, always spending more than came in. Thanks be to the Lord that my Dad never found out about the beating. Mom was right, I should have fled earlier, but he threatened me- my friends, and promised he'd settle old scores, saying he knew what people were saying behind his back. Look at me, in a refuge-a safe house. 34 fucking years old and going nowhere. Doing nothing but hide and taking state handouts. Sappho is sleeping, she smiles in her sleep. My father taught me how to fish. Sappho was so amazed and attentive when we pulled out our very first fish together. A small common Roach with little red wings. I wonder what that old guy on the opposite side of the canal was thinking.

More therapy tomorrow. I wonder where that bastard husband of mine is. I'm fed up with looking behind me- that would be the end, if he knew where...

Writing this bloody shit down don't make me feel any better- they can stuff it, what I need is a fucking big fella with fists as big as footballs. Sappho is always around since the schools have closed down; don't get any chance to meet any new guys, that's it- that's my fucking lot. 27c tomorrow fucking great.

I saw her today in the village. My fierce companion. It's because I'm looking. Loneliness is harder than I thought. She was joined at the wrist by a young girl who was tugging and pointing, falling and tripping. My imaginary companion lost it and picked the little nymphet up wholly by the hand which looked a dangerous thing to do, risky.

The village has a myriad of retail shops, pubs, restaurants, chip shops, working men's clubs. Only the larger national ones are open. The second wave of the virus has placed us back to square one. More folk are wearing masks. She was spaced out as is required outside the Chemist. I joined the queue right behind her and the little girl - knowing in my heart that if she spotted me hovering around for a third or fourth time, I would be in danger. So I broke silence and congratulated her on her fishing skills the previous day. She turned and when our eyes met it was a stare of confidence and of ease, as you do when sharing a common goal. She patronised me for a few minutes. The line of folk for drugs diminished quickly. She re-emerged from the Chemist child and prescription drugs in hand. To my surprise, as if she had forgotten, she turned and shouted goodbye. Her tired child smiled and waved to me with her limp wrist.

A week of rain, I have nowhere to venture. All I pretend I need is superfluous. Sometimes I buy for five people, forgetting. We had just got used to buying food just for the two of us, a throttling back of lifestyle.

Then she is taken from me –snatched, a fast sufferance, loss of voice, high temperature, cough, wild staring eyes, ambulance, phone calls to the hospital. Robbed.

Her clothes still hang; shoes and slippers remain where she last slipped them off. Toothpaste, shampoo, perfume, brushes, hairdryer, hobby and crafts all on show- unfinished with. I am waiting. I listen subconsciously, never hear her voice; and yet we promised each other. Simply gone. Her whole being disappeared as fast as a victim of Hiroshima. There was a very brief service at the crematorium, no hugs, or hands. Despite all her well-earned popularity we were allowed only ten mourners in the chapel-fifteen outside-understandably, just two people braved the cold and creaky transmitted service outside. The charity box on exit remained silent. Just a few scant flowers-florists shut down. Our children had driven many miles to their mother's funeral. On my insistence, they set off home. If there was a time to come to terms with being alone this was it. The house was open mouthed. I drank a few beers, dragged my hand along table tops and kitchen surfaces where she will never visit again. I have lowered my standards quickly, having not changed the bed linen. It didn't seem right-her head indentation on the pillow was still relevant. Her favourite teacup-stained brown sat waiting for the bin. I am frightened. I wake at the slightest sound. I reach for her hand and body, in my half sleep I cuddle up to ice.

I sit on the community mini bus at the back, masked and macked. Just one other passenger on the bus wearing a scarf around her mouth, there is a shortage of masks. I notice my bus pass expires in the year 2023 and I wonder deeply-don't care, not particularly interested.

Just can't see the point in these jottings, but just for the record I am worried. He hasn't seen his daughter since he was arrested. My mother said he was a control freak. Sappho asked if we were going to see her Daddy in McDonalds. Surprises me how quickly a child forgets. She was there, she saw it all! Now it's fucking McDonalds again! Too bad it's bloody closed; we could have forgotten the beating and had a Big Mac. I've had enough of bloody DVD's-TV, Internet, FB, Amazon, emails and messenger! All we need to do these days is eat, shit and piss - the money has run out! I am bloody desperate. Sappho isn't smiling in her sleep lately.

Seen that old guy again today, seems ok, nice enough, I wonder what HIS problem is?

Yesterday the sun was making up for lost time. I dressed accordingly. Made a splendid effort with the garden, mowed and trimmed the lawn. Repaired the wife's shed and re felted the roof of mine. I haven't the stomach to clean and scrap stuff from my wife's bolt hole; not yet, maybe never. I heard walkers and a few narrowboats saunter past my tow path gate. I thumbed the latch to open the gate. I hesitated. She may fishing. Lord help me, I am shying away from a situation, a title; voyeur.

My senses were overridden by a shrill scream from what I guessed from the mouth of a little girl and "Mom!" followed by a heavy wet SPLASH. I wrenched open the gate.

I saw my nymph back stroking in the canal, her daughter (with the eyes and hair of her mother) was jigging around on the canal bank, its periphery grassed as the landlord of the house owned the extent of its reach.

I saw her. She was performing back flips, breast stroke and crawl. Yellow lilies bounced with the disturbance, wild life scattered and fled, and the blackness of history coloured the water. The foulness from her initial dive had rushed to the surface. A strong odour of peat permeated the pollen rich air. All was fecundity.

My breath was shallow. I had a hollow experience in my stomach. The sight of this young woman effected my reason. She turned on a stroke and looked up into my face, smiled, laughed and ordered me to join her. I did.

It took quite a while for me to regain composure. My lack of health stood out in bold capitals. It was a stupid desperate thing I had done. My poor wife would have had me sectioned. The first virus lockdown was bad enough; a death and acute loneliness dulled my questionable intellect. Now I am taking risks, pecking at the thin shell of solitary confinement. I want to live again – greedy yes; but I will give it a shot; pour every drop of life's experiences opportunities and chances into my hedonistic soul.

This is a story on paper. Recent events which have increased the anxiety of living in a virus ridden existence is the tired and half heated issue of racism. Following a murder by a police officer in America of a black guy we see worldwide protests, not limited to major cities. Working class men and women have carried the stretcher of racism and slavery over the centuries. All skins black, white, whatever; have never quite decided where to put the fatally injured body down for Sempiternam Requiem. Benchmark for me, the poem "Strange Fruit"

So my present feelings and lonely longings story offers no race or colour. I need company in disturbing times. The young woman I feel needs company too. She has the pallor of someone who is threatened, the responsibility of looking after a daughter who is freshly exposed to the ways of men; and speaking of which, I wonder where "he" is? The Father. On paper the writer can be mean. The young woman and her daughter are – in colour. I was born in India. I am experiencing dark-"no!" black thoughts; the musings of a man who has nothing to lose, has seen it all, read too many books-weary of turmoil and conflict. She visits tomorrow. She has my co-ordinates. I have biscuits, pop, crisps and frozen chips and burgers. DVD's left over from our grandchildren's visits are scattered around the lounge.

Here I go again. I read this stuff out to my councillor. I cannot see how my miserable notes help her or me. But it's working, she can see my attitude. She just reads the stuff; it's not me responding to her-trying to be clever with spontaneous pithy remarks. I can do. I can do conversation and use big words. I'm just too fucking lazy. My first boyfriend was a clever fucker. He came from a decent family. I dumped him. There were too many bloody rules-time keeping, bus routes, dress sense, and I never felt at home in the fancy restaurants he took me. I didn't want to keep sponging off him. I preferred a coke and a KFC. I know I made a huge mistake. He smelt nice. He didn't have any tattoos. I like a bloke with tattoos. He was training to be a dentist. Met him in a rough bar. I can still remember getting some sort of kick from him being so uncomfortable. My parents were furious. My second fella had a criminal record. Then I met the bastard with the fist problem. Always blamed myself, first I stood up to him. Then the excuses and the pain scars led me to isolate and now after 7 years, I haven't budged forward. Sappho and her sleeping smiles is my only achievement-the result of an unprotected fuck. Stuck with fists. Stuck with washing and ironing his shitty stuff-the only decent thing he wears is his uniform and his hi viz. He says he will find me. I believe him, if anyone is in a position to find me it's him, and with help from his work colleagues and the lies and amateur theatricals and his innocent self-pitying, sorrowful false side…it shouldn't be too difficult. So Miss Councillor-how do you fucking sleep at night? I have the threat-you have the responsibility!

Just an hour to go. I have paced up and down the lounge for ever. I do hope they come. Just for an hour-thirty minutes-ten minutes. Long enough for me to turn back into a soft warm human. I must be measured and re assuring. I have checked the temperature of the rooms, a comfortable twenty. Double checked the stock of food and drinks. Of course I am setting myself up for a fall. She will keep away, or knock, decide, excuse and take little Sappho by the hand and walk awkwardly away. When I asked her what her name is (during that canal scenario) she said if she told me, she'd have to kill me. I am aware of what the abode on the opposite side of the blackness is used for. Yet, though I may walk through the valley of death….I will take on the sickness of her tormentor and watch her sleeping with a smile as I stand guard. Stocking my home out with necessities since the introduction of the second wave has proved problematic. Panic buying is now an art. The first wave yes, maybe understandable, but as the restrictions eased, folk have taken the piss- knowing this time what to prepare for and how relatively easy it was to stock up initially. Roads and skies have returned to whispers.

Thinking things out now. I am guessing that Mr Fists has talked his way out of his cell, knowing the system and sentences; using my non co-operation as proof of my bullish attitude, he may have been reinstated at work and is now trying to protect the public from themselves. Sappho and myself are about to pop around to the old guys home for a little break.

The visit to the old guy went well. We all wore 3 layered masks. Sappho was entertained and fed well. Whatever my little imp mentioned it seemed that he'd gone out of his way and anticipated her needs-so kind. We ate chip butties, cakes and ice-cream, watched a DVD Half a Sixpence twice! Robin is a widower. I have teased him the last few weeks. He knows my name now. Somehow his personality brings out the real me. He takes his time with stuff and is respectful of my ways and opinions. I am subconsciously learning from him like a sponge sucking up wine. It went well, but it was all so damn uncomfortable. The food was taken outside so we could distance while we ate, Robin kept deliberately distant as if his life depended on it.

Lockdown be damned. I visit my wife's remembrance spot today at the Crematorium, place a small bunch of flowers on the place where her ashes were scattered, using Battleship grid references. We walked from retirement to Covid, almost laughable, "oh the plans and the irony!" I was not alone, some way behind me waiting, my companions a victim of domestic violence and her daughter Sappho. I felt the cold wet grass beneath my feet, and I hoped Caitlin below me still smiles sweetly in her sleep. My tissue soaked up the rain that hit my skin and I felt no warmth within, only a deep dread of the future. I sensed damp warmth circling my hand. The little girl looked up from below into my eyes above and I thawed and ran down a grassy bank hand in hand with Sappho, skipping and spinning until she was reunited with her mother. I sensed the comfort of companionship; saw shimmering snapshots through the broken lenses of my eyes.

The steamy inside of the car and the sound of thrashing rain against steel enlivened my dullness. We respectfully crept on all fours away from the dreadful place; a place that manufactured stardust from loved ones and fires it into space when we aren't looking. Sappho bounced and asked if we could go to the park, the request was welcome and all agreed.

Spent the day with Robin. I wonder. I wonder what his motive is. I'm uneasy. I feel that I can trust him, but I have this feeling and at the moment I feel threatened in many ways. I need. But not this. Not this. If I stop. Sappho has taken to him, calls him Rob and he is attentive and runs like a puppy to her. Picks up things. But it's the Childs Car seat, why…on….earth…..

So we made no promises. The way of the world at the moment it's probably for the best. It was kind of her to ask if she could come along for the ride. I observed the child's behaviour. As soon as the car doors clicked unlocked, Sappho was out like a shot, followed by her mother. I strolled in the direction of my wife's coordinates, looked back over my shoulder sly. The pair stood quite a distance away. The child knelt down near a small conifer. There was a kind of familiarity about this morbid visit.

I am welcomed into this day by a tube of black toothpaste. It contains charcoal to give extra brightness.

ENTROPY

When it comes to love and finding a mate, never listen to your parents, listen to your heart. Have confidence in your ideals.

When it comes to choosing a friend,

When it comes to suffering a job you hate,

When it comes to staying up late and you feel alone in parenthesis,

Have courage to sleep in the knowledge that failures and successes will be your own.

The earth will not stop turning in your world of earning and yearning,

Above each mountain there are cloud thoughts of learning, hear their praise.

I was once an old dog trying to pull a kennel behind me,

Take down your mirrors, smash them into a skip.

Never get yourself lost amid descendants of the past,

Be found amid descendants of the future.

Fresh linen is best served cold.

Just take a look

"There's a step remember, take it slow, take my arm, can you guess yet?"

"Ok, old un, take those pennies from your eyes!"

Piss heads clap and cheer as he looks around while I lead him to his favourite seat.

A bay window bench gives ample leg room and an easy vista of punters as they arrive and depart. A slight turn of the head captures regulars sitting on stools; outside noisy traffic and industry. Above all, his chosen throne is in close proximity to the open pork crackling fire. I reach for the ale as the fusty fuss dies down; I pay and set up shop next to him. A beer, a crusty cheese and onion cob are ornaments of simpler times. I sit as usual, at his side; not face to face.

He sits and listens. Occasionally his head and body leans toward my shoulder but never touches.

He whispers,

"Who's that over there?"

"Why is there glass on the bar by the till?"

"Someone's just walked down the street with a blue mask on!"

"Somebody else has walked past with a blue mask on!"

"For a Saturday there are not a lot of drinkers"

"Well old un, since you last entered this boozer a lot has happened. I think you were last complaining about Brexit; now we have a virus to contend with"

"See this old un?"

I show him my mask. I make sure he is bought up to date.

He always complained when I took out my Android. ("I don't know why you have to keep looking at that thing!")

I show him a picture of an officer kneeling on someone's neck.

I show him pictures of rioting crowds and smashed up society.

I explain the human restrictions since the last time he was here.

I pontificate, passionate and attempt to fire up his old boiler in debate.

Too late, he weeps, the bar is silent, he fades and is gone.

NO!

One day I sat beside a stranger,
A bit uneasy,
Seemed sleazy,
A problem is best resolved speedily.

And if I were to sit beside this person again,
I would give myself in willingly,
And chillingly invite the stranger in.

I open a door using symbolic friendship.
The space behind is dark,
The darkness is replaced by a vision of a park,
I am sitting on a swing alone.
The empty swing on my right is still,
Devoid of life;
The swing to my left moves in time with mine.

A spirit whispers,
I fade,
There is darkness,
I shy away from the person;
Not wishing to share my imprisonment.
This is all I have to give to a stranger,
The gift of not knowing and loving me;
The last firework in your box.

Remember and Forget
Don't torment yourself

Enjoy the moment and press delete,

Or forever the devil be at your feet.

She was sexy, naked shameless,

And I, not entirely blameless.

Entangled, end to end,

Then a hot aching bend.

Following 50 years,

Tears from blocked tear ducts.

And from where I crouch now poised a prospect of a semi colon in parenthesis.

It has a message to send.

That this *was* serious stuff,

This shoving and pushing and arcing of one's passion,

The thrusting menu of subversive dishes,

Verses the pointless,

Act of reproduction minus the skill of seduction.

It's like eating a pack of dry stale crackers,

With nothing moving except aging knackers.

How it is,
How it was.

We never got on. Since I was 16 years old and aware of how much misery and emotional turmoil we were put through. So on this occasion I stood up for my mother. It was a very heated argument. I am an only child. I usually hid behind the upstairs landing bannister just to hear the drift and nature of the argument. When they had finished slamming doors, balling and slamming, he usually calmed down up his shed. I remained hidden in the same place because as soon as he thundered out of the house my Mother rang whoever she thought would listen and advise the most.

My father when out drinking with family referred to me as "that pratt of ours!" I knew this as uncles and friends used to tease me about it. "What you been doing to your old man then?"

These sympathetic folk knew of my father's temperament. They enhanced what I already had to put up with.

"Your dad is the only bloke in this pub who can buy and eat a packet of nuts to himself without anyone knowing. My father's parsimonious side was legendary.

I held a respectable job as a draftsman, got married, fathered 3 children, climbed up the housing snakes and ladders game. The Pratt couldn't settle. Our marriage survives till this day, my lovely wife is 63, I am 68. I am typing this in January 2021.

My Mother died when she was 89. My father died short of his 91st birthday on 21st October 2019. After putting in fifty years of surveying and estimating, on the 21st of November 2019; the day before my father's funeral I retired. It was deaths and entrances; loss of parents, and the gain of the pandemic Covid 19.

My mother was loving, until something happened. I don't know what, but in my early teens, I began to experience a separation between us. A certain coldness enveloped the home. My parents began to take holidays and park me with an aunt and uncle. I noticed movies and photos of the holidays showed a really happy couple; quite in contrast to home. On thumbing through a box of pictures and 35mm slides upon clearing their home after my father's demise, I haven't found one picture of me with them. I don't think this was deliberate but it would have been nice, just to refer to a single picture with us being a jolly family. I began to worry whilst still at home in my late teens. My mother was very attractive and on the phone following one of their "bust up's" she would often refer to two gentlemen whom she thought where making advances, gentlemen that were well off, good looking and made her laugh. I knew these blokes by sight only.

In the end she stuck it out and was loyal. (I cannot speculate, don't want to).

From the age of 16-25 the year I got married I lived in a hostile environment; I was given the spare room to set up a record player (not too loud) and a chair. My mother washed and ironed for me. The board money dates-pay days of mine, written on a Coal Suppliers Calendar. Of course mom was spoiling me with the ironing ("I'm not having you go to work or to the pub looking shabby-you need a girlfriend!")

I needed a car, my father and uncle helped me learn to drive. I passed second time. I sold my entire record collection to raise money for a 1957 Morris Minor Estate.

September 1977 I was married and housed.

My point in all this:-

It is my father I talk to now. He has been dead for over a year. I find that I talk to his ethereal presence when I need to show him how things are going here on earth.

He was very insular. In his last few years alone (Mother was in a dementia home for 7 years) I looked after his affairs - paying bills, keeping doctors and hospital appointments, shopping etc. He never weakened mentally but grew frail after mother's death. He never spoke the words I had for so long wished for, I believe this was his last hold on power.

So I say in his absence things like:-

"Dad you should see this shit, this epidemic, your favourite supermarket, I am queuing up to get in with a mask on

"Dad you are really lucky to be out of this fucking shit, you need a computer for everything (he hated technology- he had no cheque book-no bank card-no standing orders or DD's) his motto as I have stated before somewhere else in my muse; ""**Don't trust anyone!"**

"Dad you cannot get an appointment to see a doctor or a dentist!"

. The little earth to heaven snippets I try to get over to him really means he has control, he has won. I tried to get close to you during my mature years, but it went sour when their only attendance at babysitting for our three children was spoiled as a result of our being 1 hour late arriving back home on that evening of a company Xmas Party. You both wouldn't listen to our excuse. You ran from our home, leapt into your car and burned down the street in temper. We never saw you for months after.

The excuse; I like a drink; my work colleague and his partner avoided alcohol and offered to pick us up (as you witnessed) and drop us off after the party. They didn't want to leave until the death. I anticipated what your reaction would be.

You didn't let us down.

An aunt said, "The reason your mom and dad won't offer to look after their grandchildren is the furniture. They've worked hard to get their home the way it is!"

I look out from our bedroom window. It is 7am. The sky is stained heavy cotton wool winter. I see an army helicopter fly over and thunder toward an old defunct aerodrome near Walsall-delivering vaccines I guess. Its whole black image looked like a black hungry locust. I am a C.E.V. (Clinically Extremely Vulnerable); person, under the strictest of lockdown regimes. My parents were gifted 90 years, I am 68.

Analogy; Nettles are respected; Dock Leaves are ignored and trampled underfoot without a care.

It's a matter of upbringing not choice, oh! And the quality of the environment helps.

Le Petite Mort

Little death,

Antithesis,

No second, minute, hour, day.

Ad Infinitum.

This is the lesson of pausing,

Taking a breath,

Carrying on,

Knowing "little death" is D Major.

Accepting "little death" as boredom,

A Minor.

Some people are determined to grow fat in a confined space.

There's nothing at all left to be said,

I said, trying to get into my mentors head.

Whatever the battle rules of covid dictate,

It takes over our mental state;

Not knowing what day it is for one.

Will Russia's Novichok smear prompt the bomb?

We poets don't want to worry you,

We are negative capability plants who feed on facts so true.

Most thinkers are coated with insight right,

And suffer in silence and dread the night.

Now there's nothing at all left over,

Philosophers have taught..sshh!..don't bother!

In all you do

Worship the best smart inventions,

above all this,

Take time to make sense of neighbouring adverse, natural, spiralling, adverse intensions.

A Sultry Note

She is young at twenty,

Has plenty of musical talent.

Emotion cannot show through her face,

She occupies a dark place where light is absent.

I envy the girl's partner, a flamenco guitarist.

He can make a clown weep with a flick of his wrist.

Her head stretched high, her head down low,

This harpist is spiritual bordering on the ethereal.

Together, as the saying goes, they make wonderful music.

I wonder as a sensationalist

If after the recital

They make passionate love together to fuse it.

As for me,

I leave this room a cold broken string,

Utterly useless, forgotten in pain,

Never to be smeared with Rosin again.

Carious

The girl and guy left each other standing still.

Above them a Turner sky and at their feet Vincent's wheat.

The girl had been sitting at a pub bench alone.

She was using brewery Wi-Fi.

They guy with nowhere to go home saw her on his drive by.

And again; repeat.

He introduced himself.

After a while of smiles and pretence they made love on occasions of sadness on a nearby field not too far from a broken fence.

The girl and guy left each other standing still.

The linen soil beneath them was warm and accommodating. She lay naked and accepted the thrust, wriggled and gasped rolled her bust.

The guy, whilst she was riding in beatitude praised Turner's sky. The girl dug her feet into Vincent's acrid wheat, and a pact was made.

The love making was interrupted as the girl let out a scream, she explored the source that shattered her wanton dream, a rusty potato peeler deep into her back and soil; a strange object indeed - this instrument of spoil.

The girl and the guy had no better life to return to.

Two failed marriages and now all Goya and Gore. This current situation was so liquid and not so inflammatory sore.

They could not bear pretended assimilation and proceeded in a shared world of alterity.

The broken fence, sky and field witnessed cupped hands as they took the lozenges and retired forever in another land.

Nothing is more salient than companionship and death. Put these two disciplines together.

The potato peeler reveals the whole truth of purity as a result of examination and when its job is done…the girl and guy are as one and leave each other standing still.

Dawn till dust

The Earth has never been a friendly place,

So why do we bring them in?

Our Gods are at some kind of space,

So why do we bring them in?

Our food, a process of ravenous life,

So why do we bring them in?

From the time light flashes,

And the first tear drops fall;

We have cursed the little ones in our hands,

Moved on and dispersed them all.

Please read the leaflet before fucking.

Through the darkness and the wet,

We are launched innocent,

With nothing to carry,

No foe to parry,

And we are filled from syphoned poisoned vessels.

This is the process of existence,

Educated, controlled,

From an insane distance.

Launched into the arms of corruption we rest languishing and anguishing

Only the chosen are blessed with attitude.

From rude to prude, the chosen will inherit attitude.

There's only one last chord earthed mellow,

Birthed from the tunnel of a female Cello.

How I found Him
Is how I left him.

I had often wondered how it would be. He was in his nineties you see. I - an only child, old and sick. She departed eighteen months previous after a 10 year struggle with dementia.

The house, which I had become familiar with for 62 years, still stands and now belongs to strangers. I often wonder if they feel his horizontal presence in that room. His yellow tight skin, the dead face as sharp as cheese.

I rang the bell. There was a kind of inevitability I could tell. His cracked shadow didn't appear as it did for years through patterned front door glass.

It was shopping and pub day. He looked forward to it. Not a sit down visit competing with the TV, but a trip with purpose. He was a large cold sore on my lip.

I used a spare key he had reluctantly handed to me at some emotional vulnerable point. I called, "Dad!" then louder. I had practiced this for many years but under my breath and out of sight. A quick search of the ground floor rooms; I climbed the stairs in a silent cool of October lunchtime. His bedroom door was open as my vision first caught a glimpse of his head-sunken and dead in his feather bed. Then as I approached "Dad!" only softer, and when he didn't stir (I had seen him in such a pose before) I acknowledged the demise, the half-closed eyes; the jaw dropped, the sunken skin-no living personality within.

Just 18 months previous, following a long suffering, slow receding mental lucidity, my Mother died in a care home. She took her last breath between dusk and dawn. My father and the care home duty manager rang my mobile phone number for hours. Her disease took many years to accomplish the inevitable. I had grown blasé and had accepted her death prematurely as the time when she last spoke my name; the time when she shit herself in Sainsbury's-on my watch.

Changing a person in a small public toilet is not to be recommended. I struggled and after an eternity of verbal abuse and profuse flushing we got away with it.

I opened his curtains, pressed three nines.

"I have found my father dead in bed!"

"Is he breathing?"

"No!"

"Is he warm?"

"Yes, nice and comfy!"

"Do you know CPR?"

"No!

"This is what you do, and keep repeating the procedure until the ambulance crew arrive!"

My father buckled with every cross hand beat. He was warm because his electric blanket was still operating.

I was advised by the paramedic guys that it was ok to stop the damned CPR, as it appeared he was in rigor.

"How old is your father?"

"Ninety!"

Then followed the questions. The guys in green were very cool and helpful. A black van arrived, Dad was taken away. I tidied up his bed, checked that his house of some sixty two years was secure. I lingered a while-thanked neighbours who had guessed the end had come and expressed shared feelings.

Quite different to moms carting off really.

My father and I said our private goodbyes in her small bedroom. Then after some whispering we both dropped down to the ground floor reception and after a few minutes nursing staff aligned themselves into a guard of honour as mom appeared on a stretcher from a lift accompanied by two men in black. Her pitiful torso was wrapped in opaque plastic, and looked like a ball of broken branches ready for the tip.

So thus went the parenting. No final meaningful words. Their only child left empty and devoid of any passing on of wise words and gripping of hands.

I remember as a child playing in a park. The afternoon slowly began to dim, and looking around I felt lonely within. The park, once lit with white noisy voices and rejoices, all at once became silent. I sang time alone, a metronome on the only moving swing. In the distance I heard my Mother's voice creating echoes with-"dinners ready"

For the moon beer bellied in the sky as did my early morning fathers belly at dawn whilst shaving.

There was something in me. My attention has constantly been drawn to shards of other world goings on; it began when I first ventured down terraced house stairs in darkness-to the sound of snoring and the protestation of tired springs. It would be many years toward my death that I would experience a stir of what they called adrenaline.

***

It is quite a harsh reminder when loneliness peels away courage of any degree. Mortal vulnerability was rated highly by the body in the Stone Age, rage heightened the senses and spontaneously kicked started the survival engine.

Today, in the 2020 pandemic situation, we hear of lockdown folk that have, for the first time in their lives have experienced depression.

I am sitting alone. I am drinking high gravity beers in low production amounts. 330ml.

My temperament is one that enjoys company, a few pints, a human exchange to exercise the mind and consider alternate views on the way we perceive and interact with the world; but most important-laughter, cliché's, irony, sarcasm, all those characteristics that pour oil over the victims of subversive dictatorship.

We are experiencing diminished attendances at funerals. Of course nobody would use the Covid 19 excuse for not going. Certainly those who have made it into the popularity stakes and wish for a large funeral to finally get a point across, are disappointed. The anxiety of the possibility of not receiving appropriate medical treatment from the institutions we pay into is intense. The prospect of having to queue for *mundane* stuff like food is unthinkable. A shiver is experienced when at night the very idea of fuel shortages and facilities brings the mind to sharp attention when it really needs peace.

There are only illegal places to get pissed, drop inhibitions, pick up a member of the opposite sex and fuck, fuck, fuck! Musicians hibernate and die. Theatre put on shows for ghosts, the film/cinema world cease production and viewing. Can we run with normality and suffer-survive or die whatever?

I am presently similar to an upended tortoise; I will survive by a chance manoeuvre, an instinctive intervention by a normally orientated fellow, or I die by sheer inept design-responsibility God.

They were two good looking individuals. She worked in Sainsbury's in the early 50s. She caught the eye of many a male customer as she handled ham, cheese and other cold food products.

He followed in his father's footsteps and worked as a foundry hand quickly realising his skills, management placed him in the pattern making shop, where, for 50 years he became a well-respected engineer and a specialist foundry man.

From courtship to marriage and then motherhood mother worked full and sometimes part time jobs to help things along financially. Foundry work was poorly paid. Mother's jobs, telephone assembler, foundry blacker, greengrocers assistant and she still kept her good looks during work in a milliners and wedding dress shop before retiring. Her house was immaculate. His house was run with razor sharp financial efficiency.

There were many rows and mother used to *disappear* for many hours, the silence was deafening. I saw hatred in his eyes which near feeding time became a softer concerned expression. She had quite a few bolt holes to run to, he knew them all but for the sake of his manhood, refused to sink low enough to search and apologise.

Throughout their married life the argument and disappearances continued.

The marriage survived the stress. There are many holiday photos of smiles and happiness on beaches and in parks. She was diagnosed with dementia in her late seventies. Quickly her looks and charm disappeared. We tried to cope. Father and his short fuse often exploded when she refused or spat out food. It was the end; she had become an irritating object.

In contrast his demise was consisted of old age ailments, the list too boring, too groaning to paint. His body in all its headstrong loneliness let him die in his sleep.

The guy I found in bed died in my opinion with a lot unsaid which I feel is just as spiteful as his character. He left a son, a daughter in law, three fine grandchildren and a great granddaughter. Spiteful? Yes, he was hard; never praised his family if sarcasm and negativity could be used. So we went our separate ways, he left without saying platitudes and so did I. The tug of war between father and son was over. We had both reached a mutual point of exhaustion.

How I found him is the way I left him.

No child is born evil.

The struggle to *live* in adversity-

Isn't Evil, it's an inborn natural instinct for survival;

As simple as gasping for air as a church throws soil into our mouths.

Southwark Graveyard

Their existence on this traumatic earth,

Wasn't worth a fuck, according to the Church.

The cramped community piled them high and sold them cheap.

And encouraged the devil to reap and fling,

Into unmarked shit,

And that's it, that's the end of it,

Buried in unconsecrated filth pits.

Outside the boundary of a *good* ring fenced church,

There is a solitary stone.

As if she was only fuckable skin and bone,

She had nowhere to go, no family home.

You left her spirit to moan and roam.

YOU!

Bigoted, unforgiving, Christian, pretentious, piety.

Streams

I love a solitary stream.

I came across one once,

Hidden in my wondering path,

I recognised it as one I'd seen before,

At Cornwall, St Nectars' Glen.

At that place I had a solitary bath.

I checked before I self-indulged,

The Hermit wasn't present.

I took off my teenage clothes.

Threw my shyness away.

The stream was topped by a huge waterfall.

From there it ripped and rippled through a Cathedral of trees,

I waded out just up to my knees, then sat down and took a deep breath,

It was a cathartic experience, but I saved one last drop,

It's here that I wish to return,

In my doubting fearsome years.

I'm sure I will complement its flow,

With ten thousand running tears.

I like streams,

They wash the present away.

I fear that this last visit won't be the same,

As it washes me down just once again,

Much more than I can brook.

The Ultimate Lie

(To get by)

I pretended that I was happy as a child,

As demanded, meek and mild.

I pretended I was happy during adolescence,

My friends were whole, I a crescent.

I pretended I was happy as a husband, father and son,

And now the day is done.

Pretence is a weak shining light,

Darkness during the day, a crescent life devoid of fight.

I shall take this completed life back into the city,

By way of the dark entrance into births university,

A life spent in a solitary room,

My mother's womb.

What about Tuesday then?

When you realise you're nothing special,
You can shout all you want,
You're only a bobbing head in a rough sea,
Now you see me,
Now you don't.
There's other fish in the sea,
It feels too far to swim to another,
And long gone;
Are your Father, Mother, Sister and Brother.
When you realise you're nothing special,
And never will be,
You can shout all you want.
In your weakness,
You'll drift into your enemy.
Who will eat you?
Excrete you.
Now you see me,
Now you won't,
Minus
Homogenous

The Way Home

My fifty years of work.

At first I was excited at the prospect of staying away. It was part of the job. As a fire protection system designer/estimator I was given projects to design and later to estimate and tender.

1969 was all feet and inches but as months training on the drawing board passed, metric drawing submittals were required too. 1x 8th to a foot $100^{th} - 75^{th}$-50th 20th took over. Millimetres proved a little easier to calculate. 6H pencil for centre lines, 2H for general setting out. 1970 we were inking in our drawings following the pencil setting out. Pencil rubbed out, ink mistakes took a little care-being scratched out with razor blades discarded by our fathers. Set squares, 45, 60-30 and if you had the money adjustable squares every time.

"We start at 9am Steven, finish at 5.30, 2 x 10 minute breaks, 45 minutes"!" lunchtimes-hardly enough for us two trainees to get pissed in the pub which winked to us through the office window.

I cannot believe how quickly time has eaten up my working life. Calculations were performed via a log book and slide rule. Printing off a blueprint (drawing) to send for client approval was laborious. Inside a cast iron frame with arched glass, two lights hung. On top of this machine sat a long roller tray in which was poured ammonia. A window was left open behind this device as a futile effort to save our eyes.

Following the above procedure drawings hung like blankets to dry. A letter was typed meanwhile, a compliment slip thrown in too, drawings at 5pm taken to the post office and if lucky we caught the bus home on time.

My first trip was frightening. I had never been more than 130 miles- (Walsall to Barmouth- parent holidays). I had blown £50.00 on a 13 year old split screened Morris

Minor. My boss asked me to collect some cast iron valves from our head office in Radcliff Manchester and offered me 6 pence per mile. I purchased a map from a local petrol station and set off using a small stretch of the motorway M6 North and some B roads.; 200 mile round trip. I was physically and mentally jelly on my return. The valves had obviously taken me over any primitive weight limitation for my poor car. I had fought with the steering all the way back. At home, subdued, I took an early bed and slept as if I were dead.

I was once lost in the back streets of Nottingham. I drove slowly looking for a factory which should have been big enough to spot. I slowed down to a crawl. I leaned across the passenger seat, wound down the window and asked a beautiful young mini skirted girl for directions. She jumped into the car without hearing me out. A police car sandwiched me in. I did not know the meaning of the word soliciting and a phone call was made to my place of work.

We could claim expenses for meals out. I was shy, never been in café or public house on my own. My mother wrapped sandwiches in grease proof paper taken from bread loaf wrapping. I carried a satchel with a staff and measuring tape, scale rule and sketch pad and pencils. In the front pocket my compressed sandwiches suffered and were abused during a survey.

My shyness eventually disappeared.

My boss on looking at my first expense sheet; -

"What's this Steven, Chicken in the Basket and two pints of Springfield Bitter? "

I was beginning to find my feet.

During the first two years at work I found out the hard way; lessons in economics, car maintenance, sartorial presentation, office competitiveness, salary battles, fighting ones corner all this during hippy years when sex was openly discussed and presented.

In my naivety there was darkness. I felt clumsy I acted clumsy, immature and paranoid.

Although I took on the role of someone who was of average working age, responsible, eager to learn; my mind was elsewhere. I always said what I thought the recipient would like to hear. I needed to remain invisible. I simply couldn't think on my feet.

The number 6 bus took me to work and back again in the early days of officehood. Of course I spied a nice young girl and sat progressively closer on our bus stopping journeys. Never spoke. Then she wasn't there.

My parents knew the girls family (I couldn't believe I had never met her formally) and following a quick phone call, it transpired that the girl was seeing a young lad. Her parents eventually moved to the seaside and made a success running their own business. The bus girl faded away, was married and had three children before I had even got a girls feet off the ground.

I have always found the trip back home, lonesome. It's as if all my energy is taken up after sleeping, getting things done, proving I can do it, eating, bathing, putting on a suit, keeping appointments, paying my way, looking after my responsibilities; too much-oh and don't bore me with sport, and bloke small talk.

Now sixty years following the mental pressure of first day at work, I am retired. I am married, have three children and a grandchild; the way home for me remains the loneliest road.

The Character

I was shy. I'd had a girlfriend before but this girl I spied was totally different in temperament. My first relationship went well. Her parents ended it for us. This one originated in a pub, I had had too many drinks. It was a night when I had one eye on the clock so as not to miss the bus home, the other I studied the girl. She sat with two friends, the scene was exhausting to witness.

It was dark and cold outside. I popped to the toilet to save an uncomfortable journey home. I straightened myself up in the mirror and decided not to re-enter the bar, but make a dash for the pub exit-down a long paint scraped corridor.

I pushed at the wrong side of a double door to exit-fumbled, and I felt a sharp grip around my wrist.

It was a friend of the girl I fancied.

"Where the fuck do you think you're going?!"

It took a couple of nervous sentences before she let go and led me back to the bar to where I had settled most of the night alone.

She introduced herself and her two seated friends. I gave a knowing smile and eye sparkle to the girl I liked. I did what I was told and pulled up a chair. I gestured to a barmaid for another drink and offered same to the three girls, they declined.

It was all over in minutes. The three girls said goodnight and ran as fast as they could out of the building.

I had missed my bus.

I had a three mile walk to look forward to, toward the safety of my parent's home.

I knocked back the pint I really didn't want and resigned myself to the jaunt home.

To my surprise, she was outside alone drawing heavily on a cigarette. It transpired that we both had sacrificed the bus home due to mutual attraction. However she had a much longer walk home via industrial, run down areas I wouldn't have sent a marine through. Between us we had enough money for a taxi home. As we lived in totally opposite directions from the pub, only one was having a ride. I flagged down a cab. She threw her arms around me I felt her lithe figure arching against mine with vigour. Promises were made and I set off for home, my head spinning.

She was not a perfume girl. The hug had the aroma of a transport café. Her breath was smoke filled. Every sentence contained an expletive. Not the sort of girl my parents would approve of. To me, her whole presence (short that it was) was so intense, her eyes so piercing, her hair was as black as a night of serpents, and I believed she could become frighteningly addictive.

She smiled and waved from the rear church window of the taxi. The street was quiet; a chill lifted my coat collar. I found it difficult to move, I wanted to stay and wait.

Thursday was two days hence.

Mona. Mona.

I wondered why she had chosen Thursday and not tomorrow. This is how it began. A hunger lust which I had not really experienced before. My previous girlfriend was a friend first. We had been shy of performing what most of the young seventies youth took for granted. It had been an uncomfortable splitting up. The girl lived 137 miles away. Her parents - I believe- didn't want to lose her, and I had failed to get her home on time one night and that was that.

Now this girl Mona. Having listened to her conversation with her friends while I half read a paperback, she appealed to me because she said what she thought, her accomplices listened, nodding their heads.

I walked. In the solitary darkness I relived that hug over and over.

***

Thursday evening after work (and keeping the date away from parents and colleagues) I dressed a lot less smart. I had noticed the girl wasn't dressed with the thought of "capturing a bloke" in mind. As I was eager to get to know her better I put on scruffy casual stuff and waited for my mother's comment…" where on earth are you going dressed like that?"

"Darts!"

I had no intension of using buses. I parked my car alongside the pub and sat inside with the engine running. After a while I saw her two friends arm in arm and laughing and joking half skipping half walking into the pub. I wondered where my date was.

After a few minutes I casually strolled into the bar. I approached the pair of slap happy friends. They too were perplexed regarding her no show. The proffered her parents telephone number. I walked to the nearest telephone box. A deep rasping old voice answered and passed me over to the girl.

She was apologetic and skint. I arranged to pick her up on a busy traffic/railway bridge in the Black Country, some twenty minutes away. I checked my pockets; I had enough money to buy us both two drinks each. If all went well, that would be about an hour of getting to know each other. I didn't know of any easy pubs in her particular town.

I could see her in the icy cold damp distance. She was straddling a bus stop post, swinging and all bare legs. I slowed, she spied me behind the wheel and before the car stopped she had opened the passenger door. The temptress swung in wearing an icy blast and a seductive eyebrow smile. Before she spoke a word, Mona, with the dexterity of a contortionist pulled out a cigarette from a 20's box, lit it with a click, inhaled deeply and exhaled like a steam engine on a radiant.

The street was busy with impatient industrial traffic. The darkness was lit by headlights and Roman candle stars. In the dim yellow light of the car door light (which she seemed to know without thinking where the switch was) her perfectly formed legs rubbed gently together as she exclaimed how cold it was outside. Mona was wearing the same clothes she had on when I first saw her. This was a no nonsense car crash sort of girl that I had seen in films from black and white to blue. I should have made my excuses there and then. She suggested a pub. It was just a few yards from where I had pulled over to pick her up.

"Where do you live from here?" I asked sheepishly (somehow not wishing to know).

Mona pointed to a block of flats-"tenth floor-four!" We parked up at the pub she'd recommended and to be frank, judging by its outside appearance, I felt rather anxious. Her whole demeanour was strikingly sexy and before we went into the vinegar smelling bar I pulled her to a stop and offered a hug, we groped and exchanged nicotine spittle. I was too aroused really to step into the booze rich room, too happy to care.

While I pushed up to the bar between men with viscous skin and distant eyes I spied Mona at the Juke box and she sparked up the thing with the rattle of a coin and the first Chord to "Alright Now" Free.

"Who the fuck put this shit on????????.....

I nervously turned around and Mona was gesturing to the bloke with two fingers jabbing behind her back.

Mona and I talked about superficial things to a back drop of clattering shattering dominoes. After an hour I leaned over to her and whispered that I had run out of money. She stood up and gestured for me to remain seated. My little imp pushed her way through a herd of roughnecks and deftly took the hand of an old guy who looked like either a splattered caster or a crushed miner. Mona appeared to whisper in his ear, he thrust his had deep into his trousers, smiled and bid her farewell with an offhand wave.

I was hoping that the absence of money would close the date down.

I had been worrying about Mona's background and apparent day to day existence. She was loaded with energy and her rapid actions suggested she may shoot from the hip. I knew deep down that if the relationship grew serious, an introduction to my family would be uncomfortable.

I made my excuses and headed toward the gents. A cold dark corridor walk, footsteps behind me, I pushed on the door marked **Men**, the bogs smelt strong with urine, a bloke in his mid-thirties brushed against my side and wrestled his cock out to piss. He talked to the wall.

"You dating Mona?"

"Yes, met her couple of days ago!"

"Piece of advice mate, don't fuck her about, and besides do you know how old she is?"

He shook his penis, turned to me whilst I was fumbling to make myself presentable.

"What's your name mate?" he demanded with his face close to mine.

With two fingers he pointed to his eyes, then one finger pointed at me, and his last action he pointed toward the bar.

"Your girl has family in this boozer, don't screw her around!"

I pushed through the men and into the sanctuary of Mona's company.

"You've been a fucking long time!" said the smoke from her mouth.

She inhaled her cigarette hard, enough to see it being chased by its red furnace. If there was any time at all to call it off it was then. I looked through the fug of the smoke filled bar, the toilet guy was watching me. Mona crossed her legs slow and seductive; she took my hand and placed it. I was hooked. She was a stunner. Long legs, high cheek bones, 100% gypsy.

She noticed I was clock watching. She snatched at my hand, stood up sharply, pulled me through the exit, she turned into me, I put a hand on each cheek of her stone arse, we snogged, she hastily relaxed her grip with "it's too fucking cold, I'm going back in, ***ring me tomorrow!***

I heard a great uproar of approval as she re-entered the bar.

The drive home was as slow as my reasoning.

Things had been very different with my first serious relationship. The girl's family were polite and welcoming, her father a military man. My coat had been stolen from a hanger in a lovely village pub. By the time I'd phoned the police…anyhow I got her home late. No second chances, it seemed all too convenient, a sudden termination of a serious courtship. I had a long 3 hour drive home. Her father wrote to my parents to twist the knife….it was all over in a couple of intercepted love letters which as her father said only proved my arrogance and disrespect. My parents had met my distant girlfriend and had approved. However it was pointed out that her parents would have objected to her leaving her town 135 miles distance to set up home with me. So the break seemed very convenient indeed.

I had failed to ask Mona her age but guessed she was under the legal age for drinking and shouldn't have been in the boozer. I wasn't too sure if I should continue with Mona. In fact all things considered the bloke with the big dick was flagging up the possibility of trouble. Sexual attraction, sexual attraction, thrusting embraces and the feel of her body and the taste of her nicotine lips and…and…and…she outweighed me on courage…she shot from the hip alright, I was as weak as a failed diplomat. I needed a partner with strength and worldly wisdom. Love making would be the clincher.

The next day in the office I picked up and dropped the phone a few times. I was still short of money. The burden of car ownership and sartorial awareness was taking its toll.

All I had to do was absolutely nothing. I could stop worrying about family introductions. I could clear my mind; stop lying about my movements. It was if Mona was *sent* to me during my constant sulking self-indulgence regarding my first love and loss. Mona was a million miles from the character played by the first lady. Mona was an enigma, a young girl caught in a tiny industrial poverty stricken world. I made up my mind to ring her. I needed to know what I was letting myself in for. I had to meet her parents and make an assessment of the situation. I felt I had let my own parents and my first girl's parents down. I should have behaved more measured; but at the time I felt rejected and as this was a negative feeling; I rebelled against the suggestion that it would all blow over. I was broadsided. I was depressed and angry so after a few pleading unanswered letters to Suffolk I took a swig of beer alone and said ***fuck it, fuck them!***

I didn't find out until a few years after the split that the distant girl and her parents had been writing to me…my parents reading the letters and hiding them. My mother admitted this on the morning of the day I was to be married.

***

I rang Mona's number. A gruff grandmother of a voice answered.

"Who's this?"

"Paul, can I talk with Mona please?"

I could hear the TV in the background, a cough, a sound of dishes arguing, laughter, then:-

"Paul, I don't have money, its fucking hopeless at the moment"

"Can I come and pick you up?" "I know a social club and it has a great jukebox, my uncle drinks there!"

I had asked for a sub from my boss, so was eager, champing at the bit. I couldn't bear spending a night in watching the old slap on the side TV- with twisted coat hanger aerial.

Mona agreed.

I parked outside the named block of apartments and with mixed feelings I spied her hovering about in the ground floor foyer. I had hoped to meet her parents. She ran to me as I opened the car door, it was a windy night she was wearing a most orgasmic red mini skirt and a yellow silky top under a grey greatcoat.

"I saw your car at the lights from the balcony Paul, pressed the lift!"

I didn't need to smoke as one nicotine snog from Mona melted me. We spent time at the social club, my Uncle liked Mona a lot; in fact they both got on like a house on fire. He squeezed a couple of quid into my hand with... "make the most of life Paul, take her for chips!" I thanked him. Little did he know that I had been duplicitous in my motive to use his club. I desperately wanted to let my parents know I had another girl. When I returned home later that evening there was a light still on; I knew my plan had worked. My uncle had given the game away and gave my parents big thumbs up for Mona. My only concern was he was something of a flirt and Mona had been dressed rather provocatively. I had to give it a try though.

"Courting again we hear!"

It was late and I was relieved that mom and dad had decided it was too far into the night to give me the third degree. The next few weeks where full of;-

"And when are we going to meet this girl?"

I stretched this particular request so far into the future-my parents along with an aunt and uncle, tracked Mona and I down to a basement heavy rock evening at a town centre venue. I had mentioned that it had become a regular venue to my flirtatious Uncle. The Cellar Club was in no way a place for parents. They had been so frustrated at not having the opportunity to interview Mona that it had come to this. Fortunately it was eye contact only as the place stank of beer and weed and the oldies pushed past and retreated back upstairs and onto the road.

The weird thing is; Mona and I had not, after six weeks of heavy petting, suggested to each other... a parent meeting. I sadly suspected that Mona was embarrassed about her parent's circumstances. I was wary of my Mother and Fathers possible reaction to an uncut diamond of seventeen; who smoked with lungs that could suck a man's shirt tail up his arse.

***

As our friendship developed I picked up a kind of sensibility in Mona. I guessed that she may be fighting shy of meeting my parents and was only too aware of her social standing. There was more to Mona than met the eye. When I suggested that her reluctance may be because she was nervous; her hard Medusa persona, melted into tears with volcanic energy.

On this date we agreed that we would socialise with our parents soon, (my mother and father had complimented Mona on her good looks following the cellar debacle).

To keep up financially with regular courtship I had been putting in some overtime. I treated Mona to some clothes and selfishly suggested sexy stuff, of course she agreed and her eyes shone like gilded China cups. I was no longer shy or embarrassed when she swore in public places.

Mona secured a full time job in a local factory as a packer of hardware into brown boxes. Mona and I took it in turns to finance our nights out. I met her parents finally by organised accident. We drank locally-by her homestead one night and my home town the next. Mona and I walked into a tiny boozer that was heaving and heavy with smoke. Mona grabbed my hand, and pulled me through a busy crowd onto neutral ground and introduced me to her parents. An intense ten minutes suddenly escalated into an amicable couple of hours. We dined proudly on cheese and onion cobs and crisps. Her parents looked the same age as my deceased grandparents, I put this down to cigarettes and alcohol. The four of us were tired of table tennis forced platitudes and eventually scrummed ourselves out into the cold dark industry of the Black Country. In the distance stood my girl's block of flats all lit up like a Chinese lantern.

"You get off home Paul, I'll walk with my mom and dad, and I have promised them chips!"

I wiped condensation from the inside of the car windows-we had made love on the back seat earlier, and as I drove home I wondered why I was dismissed from the rest of the evening so casually.

My parents met Mona on neutral ground. They habitually had a drink with friends in a mellow respected social club.

Unbeknown to Mother and Father Mona and I had joined the club many weeks previously and were known as regulars; thee two of us despised the folk who were upset when we sat in "their" seats. The stage was set, we stormed trooped my parents rabbit hole on their favourite Friday night; it was their turn to feel awkward.

Mona was scantily dressed and shone with wanton sex appeal. The conversation was extremely awkward as I had planned. My parents drank with two other couples of the same age and class. This broadside idea of mine backfired with devastating consequences.

That evening after I dropped Mona off at her flat, I drove home feeling pensive and a feeling of hollowness devoured me.

I let myself in to my parent's house, hung up my coat. The lounge door snapped open.

"Keys!"

My father demanded and I handed them over. I pushed past him to question mother. It was obvious she had been crying.

"It's her or us!"

A suitcase was flung into the hallway by my father. My mother wiped her eyes with her sleeve…but at no time did she come to my rescue.

I slept at work and colleagues houses for a time. Relatives had been pre warned not to take any notice of my bleating.

It was impossible.

I made a choice that made me feel wretched for eternity. I hadn't enough money to put petrol in the motor. I caught the bus to date Mona. She asked me what the matter was as I had been quiet all evening. She bought me another drink.

"You'd better go home to your Mom and Dad after this!" She said.

Outside that boozer, I said goodnight. It was cold, and in the distance I saw my bus which was like a great shining chariot-blasting toward me. We kissed for the last time. She turned and ran back into the bar. I wanted the earth to swallow me up. Reality took me home.

I knocked on the door of my old man's house…..

Buried my head in a pillow and howled and howled a cry of utter defeat, utter fucking defeat….by the hands of parents who thought they were Gods.

Being Dead

Life is just a row of fucking ducks. Yellow - they pass at shoulder height to God. Some get blown to bits by a sawn off shotgun, never knowing where the fuck that fucking came from. Some pass over with a clean shot on the back seat of a bus - top floor. Some poor bastards are victims of shoddy shooting; they being picked off slowly, hanging on, hoping and praying profusely to invisible gods and doctors. Those who survive the dash know that they will soon go around again; until eventually, they too get the options.

I came out of the darkness and back into the light on many occasions. I was a martyr to entertainment. The light dimmed as I went around for another spin, then "Bang!"

I wasn't at all bothered. Life was too complicated anyway. Having been born by plastic moulding machine in the early 1950's – the good old days when TB patients where head outside and body in. Now on the certificate at £8.00 per copy it said multiple organ failure, dementia, "old age" 20/02/2000, three little ducks and some Japanese Zero's.

There was this sigh, the end was nigh, I looked out of the window at the sky and picked my time to bastard die. I gestured the best I could with the brain as thick as mud, to glass and asked a pretty masked girl who I thought was my daughter for a glass of water. This fucking blithering idiot, with a soul of shit, made a last will attempt at ending it, and took my last breath into the depth of darkness.

Duck gone.

There's a lot of bloody speculation as to what we move into in respect of passing over. I was happy to realise that a stupendous sensation of negative capability ensued. A dark tunnel? Yes! there certainly is. Welcoming friends and relatives? Only when willed. When one passes over there is a deep timeless sense of peace. Of course there's no physical body. I've floated around here now long enough to know that those who die before they have gained a personality are sent back.

So I became an entity of eternal ethereal existence. At first there is a strong instinct; a wish to talk and cuddle mother. Then another wish; a yearning and longing to speak and exchange non existences with anyone that springs to mind. Take it from me. If you want to speak to Adolf, Mata Hari, Jimi Hendrix, just roll out their names they will be there. Communication is easy it just enters the mind and bang! Heavenly Bluetooth.

That's what folded my mind in; all that earthly human bollocks - technology. Computers, cards, games, satellite navigation and the biggest mind blowers of all-too much choice and corruption.

Glad to see the fucking back of it. As far as love and sex is concerned on earth they are different entities. With the emphasis on the tities!

Regards,
Jim the Dead.

When I was alive I often wondered if spirits could visit and message the living. The answer is yes, but this depends on how *aware* or how *receptive* the targeted human is. I have often willed a visit to my remaining family, pub, and workmates. They are all there. I cannot influence them. As in the haunted movies I used to watch, I can make objects move, I can materialize, but to be frank – it is that strenuous it's hardly worth the effort. Making a mate shudder at a bar when he's ordering a pint is too tiresome. Yes the dead have energy, the energy is light;

one can exhaust the supply of light. Space is an absolute miracle. I have talked to particles, spun down black holes, followed twisted light highways. Being dead is very lonely, but the experience is so overwhelming and intense I hope I don't get posted back to that nasty planet. The human being has evolved to a point now that they are inventing systems they deem necessary - only to find they cannot control them.

I was in a way glad that my death came when it did. As I said my mind was buffering and I felt – rather knew - that I had absolute no control over things that once came natural.

I do long for company; Interaction with the opposite sex for instance; handling of a warm hamster, and buying a round of drinks.

I am tired now. My light is diminishing. It will be some time before I have the dusty energy to communicate again. There are many deaths, even when one has been destroyed by the incinerator. This in itself was a horrific experience.

I saw the vision of my body bursting.

Must go now, I am weak.

I did see my mother.

I reached out for her. She backed away and was gone.

Now I don't understand, never will, the light is not to be used for sentiment.

PS Never judge a person from the way they present themselves. It's what you don't see which is the truth, the way, the light, reason and the result.

Dust the bloody spare room!

Hope you found these messages ok.

See you soon

Jim the Dead.

Cello

In my humble opinion there is no other instrument that produces a haunting soul torturing sound as the Cello.

I am a blues fan. It all began in 1967. Looking back it was on the cusp of Black and White and Colour. In 2021 I feel compelled to dedicate a part of me to a modern day virtually indestructible flash drive.

I have been wasting money for over 50 years collecting music recordings. I have been hiding behind hoardings hoping not to be found out. From the early days of Eric Clapton until the more recent rise of Joe Bonamassa I have adored string bending.

As in a lot of sad cases, it was the Woodstock festival that blew the lid off blues spectators e.g. Jimi Hendrix and his rendering of the Star Spangled Banner. The void which he left behind has only part been scaffolded out.

A discovery via a David Lynch film, Lost Highway of a tenner sax player meant that there was a lot of hidden talent out there and I set out to investigate.

You see, for me music, draws out the soul. It does this to fans of many music genres. Music is one of two international languages, the other being mathematics.

The depressing poetry and guttural fag smoking tone of Marianne Faithfull has meant that I have all her widely available recordings.

For deep blue's rifts I chose Henrik Freischlader and for mind blowing abys stuff Nick Cave.

At the end of my life cycle however; No other instrument will accompany me into the dark depth below.

The Cello.

The guitarist's way to please a master Baker

When it comes to sex and you need to know,

Which end to start from, head? Belly? Toe?

Try kissing her passionately on the lips,

Give your hands something to do.

Stroke her like a feather on her hips, until things begin to grow.

It's like baking a fine loaf of bread,

Knead her body fill her with yeast,

Pause shortly and increase the heat.

There's a lot of agitation, and the heat is hot,

Now she'll show all that she's got,

Don't forget to tune her up,

Pluck her hard and just add a little more,

Use your fingers and cunnilingus,

Flip her over, bend those strings,

Turn up the volume, until the feedback sings

Now that things have finished being slutty,

Take her to the chippy and buy her a butty.

To a friend I never knew

Finish off that beer my friend,

Now the wait is over and you've had a few.

Again and again you have looked at the clock,

Sighing while musing about bad things that shock.

I'm sorry that I couldn't remain alive,

To share a beer with you,

That thing was too strong for me,

It may be too strong for you.

Go!

Move on to somewhere, someone new,

Go!

Take up your coat, clear your throat,

Bid me Adieu!

\For I am too sensitive to see you weep

And all I need this minute,

Is a hand of darkness to soothe me to sleep

Howling

When the epiphany reveals,

the inability to live with oneself,

And it's impossible to wholly resurrect the thrill

One is nothing,

Two is one,

Three is too many,

Because

You are out there somewhere,

And I love you still.

I want to walk

I want to walk,
Like times gone by.
I walked as a young man should
With head held high.
I want to walk,
Like I met you proud,
Head in the clouds,
Turned bright blue sky.

And I want to sing,
Like times gone by.
Sing again like an old man should,
Looking at the earth below
Friends that never said hello,
offering the stuff I never could,
And I want to sing
I cannot cry.

I love you and I love life,
I don't want the time again,
I just want to walk,
As I remember you,
By your light,
That lit up the coldest night
I just want to walk.
We don't have to talk.

De Profundis
From the Depths

This is a product of being isolated due to Covid, it is 3rd Feb 2021. For 12 months this loneliness spells seems to be growing longer. Friends have nothing new to communicate. Fake news means we cannot rely on anything we're being told; conspiracy theorists are making life difficult. I have always felt that a community cannot survive unless there is trust. It is now obvious that slow deliberate action may be paying off regarding a vaccine. Another of my own personal beliefs is that it is better to go down the wrong road rather than let other people make the decision; indeed it is better than staying still. So below this introduction is a disjointed recording of what I threw down during a chilly afternoon in my man cave drinking until pissed. It is shattered thought.

First can of honey lager from Poland….Is sin a sickness?

Playing Citizen Cope:-Sons Gunna Rise.

How can we live a pious life? – A life using humility as a taught attitude.

I am interrupted, a beer delivery by a Black Country Brewer, Fixed Wheel.

Should we try to live and study piety? It is over 2k years plus since Socrates tried and as a consequence was accused of corruption of the young?

The declaration of human rights offers well thought out words; a way to behave for states and citizens. I wonder about the guys who have signed up to this, they are either bearers of blind eyes or gifted with a third eye.

How can we erase smugness?

The vision of a CEO in all his private plane ebullient freedom during the epidemic; breeds unrest. If something doesn't feel right it usually isn't.

How can we change for the better?

Four empty cans, no knock at the door from Amazon, no post, no meaningful social media, no phone calls, every horizon looks the same. May as well remove the hands from the clock, take all batteries out, take the batteries out, I am now considering to take my own batteries out.

How can we improve?

By studying historical writings - autobiographies.

By being brave enough to be alone.

By not fearing that one is different from others, e.g. not going with the flow-stoical

By being a free agent in all seasons.

By accepting that death is the master; not life.

I reach for the last drink of the afternoon, I have lockdown rules. See the black dog licking the patio glass, and that's me lot!

And most important………

A GLOBAL RESTRICTION OF NUMBERS - A REDUCTION OF HUMANS FEEDING ON THE SORE TEAT OF MOTHER EARTH.

I have a secure but negative feeling, come to think of it, I cannot remember, an instance in the past 50 years, when someone asked my opinion.

A Sprinkle of Darkness

There was this old lady. She sat by my mother depending upon the order they encouraged them in.

The establishment possess more females than men.

I have from childhood been an observer rather than a participant.

My mother is dressed depending upon the order clothes as they rubbed their eyes. It doesn't seem to matter. Once, way back in the sixties and seventies it did matter. Mother took pride in herself. Now she sits awkward in an awkward chair which has no particular place and rests on a carpet, the pattern and colour of which nobody cares about, no one remembers, it's a carpet, Mother is a female. The male sits between two ladies.

Through a slice of an unsecured door drifts a smell of over- cooked everything. There will not be starters. Mains are uniform and mostly remain on plates posing as soft décor looking up at a magnolia ceiling.

There is this old lady slipping down away from her food. Her unsettling performance is a regular ritual; bed, lift corridor, seat, slapped meal, wriggle, slide and floor.

A young nurse pushes assistance away coldly.

"Let her be, let's watch and see!"

Old lady crawls across a surface thick littered with limbs and wooden legs.

A young nurse is crawling on all fours following and mimics.

The lady struggles to the upright piano; slaps the lid open, and her skeletal figure plays the Dream of Olwen.

I remember, a wise person, in a cancer ward. His words, "Beware of friends; most are spiders, you will be imprisoned in their personality webs, they will say the things that comfort you, but the motive here is a cheap meal, they will suck you dry and leave you hanging in an arid and obscure place until you resemble carapace!"

These things drift through my mind as I sit clock watching, watch watching among folk who are queuing up at the despatching home. They wait; with nowhere to go - all phases signed off, risk and method statements sleep tucked away on obscure computer systems. Close relatives as weary as brown leaves flutter through the home and sign a visitors book; embarrassed with a truthful time in-time out time but at least they made an effort.

The rest room is all broken sticks and false smiles. The aroma of kitchen repeats a burp of exhaustion; time for slush puppies of breath giving spoonful's of mush without room. It's a job. It's a parking of bodies. It's all there is left, sores, aches, meaningless stimulation, only a few really want to be absorbed into the mystery of dementia. A good week is defined by the turnover of inhabitants, the vacation of stiffs, the cleansing of bedrooms, the stability of constant custom and employment.

Sad clothing hang like a poet's strange fruit from hangers in musty wardrobes.

It is 66 years since the woman by my side spat out my vulnerable frame.

The date my terror began in light was 21/11/1952.

They said to start in the middle, then a backstory, and follow the middle to the end.

So I sit here in a care home. Things are running through my mind, overthinking; a modern term. I am thinking of closing everything down. It has to be a gentle process, so stealth like that nobody will notice. It's quite natural, as we age, close down, until our spirits escape and wait for an open window through which to drift into the dark eternity.

I have tried to be true, attempted to be virtuous.

I joined a fraternity, the buffs; it took me 40 years to re name it - hypocrisy. Since resigning, no brother has contacted me to ask why.

I served as a licenced Lay Reader in a Christian Church for seven years, until I felt the pain of Christ turning in his grave. No worshiper from the church contacted me to ask why I had handed in my surplice and cassock.

Social media has given me much pain and pleasure. That is until a younger family member publicly summed up my character and assassinated it. Totally wrong; absolutely did not know me as a person.

So it's time to close everything down, close everything down, close everything down-Dead.

1957

She, nanny, sips on her tea,

Her stockings uneasy around the knee.

And me a fifties child.

He's grandad, dunks a poker in his beer,

And rolls another cigarette spear.

And me a fifties child.

She, mother, pulls at her hair,

He, father wishes not to be here.

And me a fifties child.

There's lamb gravy stained plates in the kitchen,

And a dog that never ceases itching.

And me a fifties child.

A dripping tap, a whistling kettle,

There's nothing present willing to settle.

And me a fifties child.

Wrist baring watches are lifted and ditched,

It looks like rain; it's going to rain,

The few words are not in vain,

Prompts hats and coats on,

Candles are blown out and someone shouts out,

See you in the New Year no doubt.

The fifties child cries.

Aside

Rich people set the bar too high for genuine friendship to flourish.

Shit!

I am being chased across a huge field of Barley. Behind me; a flock of youths are shouting and threatening; I start to run.

Suddenly-above and behind me, a noose approaches fast. The noose is tethered to the skids of a helicopter I cannot see the pilot. The opportunity is too good to miss and as it overtakes me, I run, dive and shoot my arm awkwardly through the roped loop.

I leave the ground at a terrific spiteful speed. The mob below grows quieter and smaller as I am thrust toward heaven. As I am hoisted my heart and lungs reach bursting point. I am in terrible pain due to the awkwardness of my tethered arm. I hang and dangle at increasing altitude.

For the life of me I cannot understand what had prompted the mob to be angry at me vigorously. I am confused as to my timely rescue by a helicopter. The incident happened so suddenly, yet not resolved. My pain is so intense now that I fight to stay awake. I am calm and realise that I am in total control of this situation.

I struggle to free my arm. I still cannot make eye contact with the pilot, we are descending, I am in control I struggle and succeed in freeing my arm. The pain is gone and as I see the earth growing near. There is no pain, as I fall, I see below me a huge dog dragging a child through crops.

Corruption unbridled.

I'm not in a rush and won't beat about the bush.

There's always something to be said about our fellow men.

Whether or not they're dead, failed the test, tried their best

All the food a bottom line human can eat,

Doesn't lie at piety's feet but at the behest of a person making a judgement on what feels right.

From murderous rival's hands

And common through earths lands

There are gestures and postures.

Warning, enticing, mourning and rejoicing; trust lies thin.

A new born child carries the potential

To command heaven and hell,

All our lists, genres, religion, arts, crafts and science, transmit disease;

Two common languages, Music and Arithmetic can be trusted,

in order to develop these two,

basking in the light of truth they portray,

every day we feed from hands

of corrupt unaccountable impious men.

Don't worry its mandatory.

The Lachrymose Labyrinth

Suddenly things aren't what were expected.

The clapping faded away….a few strides from reception,

Rejection and a grey summer's day fresh air.

Bed then retirement.

Slowly as the curtains of the mind open it dawns, it's only

Yawns from now on.

Sixty lashes of reality wakens the weary dead,

And nothing left to dread.

Sixty lashes of reality wakens the weary head,

Tested, ingested, spat out, this winner of bread.

An old oil cloth of a worker,

Beaten, useless-no berserker-no shirker.

It is impossible to track down one's life, nobody cares, they'll flick through your CD's swinging the bag, bumping their knees, carrying your shirts and shoes in pairs.

It doesn't matter no more, no more,

Which way around you hit the ground, you've finished standing upright!

You gave it your best shot, someone else threw in the towel.

Say goodbye to self-respect, follow the lights of the night

Never no more circumspect.

On exit you will be alone. Maybe someone trying to make conversation will say,

Remember

The Long Walk Alone.

When I was an island,
In a playground,
I looked for a Brother.

When I was a teenager,
I looked for a Brother,
When I had health issues,
I looked for a Brother.

When I worked hard and fed a family,
I looked for a Brother.

When, on the day of my retirement,
I looked for a Brother;
I saw my reflection in a shop window,
And realising the epiphany
Echoing my solitary years,
I had, all that time,
Been dressing a Manikin.

Diamonds running down a Black Pane

When my mind decides to play tricks,

And all around is Stedman six,

My hand usually hangs in bedside bric a brac,

Spider fingers search for books, pellets in tins, cd's and things to anchor me into this,

This detritus world, white and black.

When my body prefers to rest,

And bones and muscles are past their best,

A cage covered in thin pale skin drum taut,

This is not my end, only a tug of a rope,

Timing is everything,

I lie naked,

A perfect trope.

It came to pass

Just a few months before I found my Father dead in bed I had taken him to Barr Beacon. He was 90 and really too weak to step outside of the vehicle.

I parked the car on top of this high point in the Midlands, betwixt Aldridge and Birmingham. I chose a spot that gave him a good vista of Walsall; behind us, so we are told, if the earth was flat we could see Russia. Our windscreen faced in the direction of the Wrekin and on to Wales.

Dad asked why I had chosen to come to this place instead of our direct drive to the pub in Walsall. I lied and made a remark about a bit of fresh air. In truth I was exhausted and needed a break and the Beacon had been a place of pleasure in my childhood (flying kites and balsa planes). I knew he and Mother had often walked here and loved the place.

I had actively helped my parents in any way I could during moms many years of dementia; right up to her death. Tired, depressed and at a loss in regard to Dads predicament, I took part in a remember session. I pointed out key points, St Mathews Church, Aldridge Airport, East Arboretum, foundry chimneys, reminded him of the pubs he used to drink in.

Dad kept looking at his watch.

"Have we time to go to the Royal Oak?" he said.

I took him to the Royal Oak.

"Have we time to go to the Rose and Crown?" he said, as we drank in the Oak.

Can you take me to the Red Lion?"

And on it went until I asked, "Dad, what are you looking for?"

"I'm looking for old mates" he snapped.

We ducked into the car again; I drove for five minutes and pulled up outside the entrance to Ryecroft Cemetery.

I had gambled on my assumption that we both retained our wicked sense of humour.

It paid off, how we laughed.

Creative Posing

A poem here a short story on its way,

Said she'd laid down a play the other day.

Stage or Radio?

She didn't say.

Our superior woman taking tea,

Took a liberty - disliking me.

So full of herself,

So empty of kindness;

I suspect her book at the publisher,

Will be quite spineless.

At that Point

It was at that point in the road.
I looked up and across at the Care home.
Uncontrollable tears flowed.

It was at that point I spied the window
That let the light into my Mother
I often opened this and let a gentle breeze flow.

It was at that point in the traffic jam.
I felt inadequate as a son,
A poor excuse for a man.

I had helped my father park her there.
Into a place of strangers,
Was this questionable act of compassion fair?

Motive is more complex than a spider's web.

They opened the window to let her out
I am imprisoned in my head,
She has gone forever no doubt.

We are all caged in a mental cell
And at this point of realisation
I know at the time I didn't do very well.

A Fist full of face Masks

When during lockdown you have a list of tasks,
And upon arriving at the superstore there's nothing in your pockets but masks.
This is a sign of memory loss; we are supposed to chuck used ones away,
Yesterday has gone now; when the shopping list went astray.

The petrol tank is dreadfully low,
Your blood pressure dangerously high,
On line banking and prescriptions should help to ease the flow,
Card only sir, Cash only sir, enough to make you cry.

You wonder what day it is and what was it that you missed?
Did you do it yesterday? Or was it the day you got pissed?
You pick up the phone to speak to a mate,
He doesn't answer just great!

When this is all over,
And if you can still remember your name,
Don't let reality takeover, hang on to that hangover,
Let someone else bask in your shame

LD2

There's too much beer,

Too many bottles standing near.

This 2020 human surprise,

Has opened up many blinded eyes,

I cannot guess now,

What the future will decide.

Can't take the machine,

Can't take the ride.

I shall open up another bottle or two,

Sit in darkness thinking of you.

And hope that someday we shall be free again,

See again,

Feel again,

Freedom

A blind man and woman,

Lost in the garden of Eden.

The Lost
2020

I have not heard the whisperings of religion,

Or felt the grip of a strangers soul,

Or inhaled the scent of spring,

Or read words from wise men and women,

Or tasted a bitter pill,

Where is the deity?

Why are we all so ill at heart?

Autumn Leaves 2019

I stepped down from the train, fifty years of work over. I joined a shambled queue. Ceased being an estimator rover. A taxi I called with a gesture picked up someone else. A bus roared and edged out from the transporter hub. There was a thinning of commuters. This was all new to me these bikes, trams and scooters.

The company car had been inspected and re-possessed. I handed in my surveyor's equipment like a sheriff tossing in his badge. Having lightened the load - just a late November coat to cut the wind; a suit shirt and trousers to be parked.

I tapped to check the wallet was there.

In my solitude among a hundred thousand ants, I pushed to a bar realising as I stared wide eyed from a bay window, I had finished the dance; unbeknown to me the world had also pulled into my station and was committed to a mysterious sanquination.

Tomorrow, Eulogy for my father and I anticipate a mood following the service. I expect to feel absolute loneliness now that both parents have gone. I shall have no recourse to blame them for any stupidity or errors of judgement from now on. I will turn away from the light, listen to a little blues number-Nobody's Fault but Mine, letting the song dribble from a nearly silenced music system in my man cave.

From my left hand I have in the course of two days have dispensed with over a hundred work colleagues and customers. My right hand is hanging onto a much reduced world, my wife and children and a small circle of drinking friends.

Walking into our garden to sigh, I see nothing but pressed flowers and weary herbs, vines and trees.

As much as I tried I was never destined to be a bestselling CD, and would be happy now being as a dog eared Music for Pleasure LP.

Ten Covid months have passed, and although I have hung my hair from a semidetached turret window, I have not been rescued. Stupidly I long to leap back onto the train to the office; coward I know, no doubt about it, but I no longer have the strength to see my loved ones left over without.

The sea hits the harbour wall plumes and rages to the sky in a smashed wave, fragmented it falls back and is lost. If nothing matters it is life itself. A sense of the *self* is utter delusion. "Nemo Mortalium Omnibus Horis Sapit" (no man is at all hours wise). The population of the world finds itself once again threatened by a pandemic and we are divided right down to the last denominator.

Today the words "hope and trust" seem to be very popular. Following fifty years as design, site surveyor, and estimator of fire sprinkler systems in all honesty I was never keen to embrace advances in technology. I began on the drawing board with a pencil, rubber, pencil sharpener, set squares, log books, scale rules, wooden measuring staffs and cloth tape measures to 50 feet. This was late sixties. My entire career I sensed that if this primitive way works why mend it. Today we rely on computers, and hidden systems. We can be exposed to helplessness in seconds.

I hate the feeling in the pit of the stomach when things go wrong.

Sorry we don't accept the card. (No gas and electric).

This Post Office will not be open on…..

Sorry, No Diesel, (a ride and eventual queuing elsewhere)

There has been some activity on your…..is this you?

Cashpoint out of order!

The progress further please visit our terms and conditions

Other things, Internet down, router fault, please sign up to Patient Aid for all your Doctor's appointments and prescriptions…

Due to high demand you are in a queue, please leave a message so we can ring you back, due to high demand you can expect a wait of 40 minutes….

Outside banks in the line of helpless victims… What are you waiting for? I want to make a deposit and send some money to…please go on line…haven't you a relative who can help?

For God Sake, how did we fucking get here!!!!!!!!?

Hidden corporate shitheads must be laughing at our vulnerability because we are all too dumb to set a fucking password, tick how many fucking squares hold a picture of a traffic fucking light, cannot remember a favourite poet or our grandmothers preferred style of underpants! Go on a nice touring holiday in Cornwall; let's see how you cope with paying for car parking!

To end this diatribe; I haven't seen many religious/religion based representatives on TV or Radio.

Long live chaos, Death to spirituality!

"And where do you see yourself in the next ten minutes?"

"Just relax and tell me what sort of guy you are!"

Well to be truthful I suppose I'm an **A**verage sort of guy;

Quiet harmless, inoffensive, kind of **B**enign at times.

I have, in the past, I know, have been used as **C**heap labour.

Because of my mild manner folk have **D**espised me; inferior.

I suppose I come across as **E**mpty, senseless; devoid.

I'm not particularly **F**aint hearted or weak. I suppose though

I may at times be **G**ullible, but in no way dim or pale.

On some occasions, I wish for praise, but too **H**umble-modest.

I often feel out of place, a bit clumsy, **I**nept, but happy.

A can be a little **J**aundiced in the workplace and socialising.

I am riled at the sight of someone **K**owtowing to superiors.

Most of all I love being kept busy love being **L**aden with stuff.

Hate **M**audlin colleagues, they act with too much sentiment.

Best way forward, work hard, pretend one is **N**othing, amen.

Ok, I think I have told you enough to sum me up as **O**btuse.

We all have our peccadilloes, I am a **P**arsimonious bloke.

Yes I like a beer or two, helps **Q**uaff away tense moments.

Too true, I am a decent conservationist, have studied **R**eason.

I think I would make a good **S**emicolon, give and take-ease.

As far as I'm concerned, never partner me up with a **T**ardy.

Give me a lot of work; I'm fucking brilliant at being **U**biquitous.

I like strong captains at the management wheel - no **V**acillation.

And don't team me up with a bloody puritanical **W**owster.

Put me with any customer I am not in the least **X**enophobic.

I can think out of the box and have a **Y**en for finding the truth.

Just to sum me up then, I am a product of the **Z**eitgeist-fin.

"We'll let you know!"

"Goodbye!"

"Well?"

"There's just something about him I cannot put my finger on!"

The Wood for the Trees.

My apprentice and I were drifting through a lovely little wood at the side of an old airfield. It was a crisp spring morning, blue skies, busy with birds. We could hear heavily drenched grass flicking at our boots. The air we breathed had a sort of metal nose to it and a sharp temperature.

My pupil said she was glad I knew the way. We had no plans. So we meandered from a long abandoned Second World War runway across a field and into a little wood.

Sappho suddenly gripped my upper arm, and gestured to keep halt and keep quiet.

"Theo standstill and listen!"

A gentle breeze rustled the trees, and as if we were under threat, we fell to our knees and Sappho whispered.

"There's someone crying in the distance!"

Sappho sure had a keen ear which is a good asset for folk in our line of work. As I was getting on in years I let her carry on describing the soulful sound and direction until she grew impatient and ran. I hardly kept up with the agile girl. Gradually as we lumbered through thick and threatening undergrowth we suddenly halted before a wailing, crying and sobbing guy. He was seated with an arm around a young silver birch tree. His eyes sore red, hair dishevelled. He appeared to be of retirement age.

I made a decision to let Sappho take control of the distressful scene.

I crouched; then sat with my legs dangling in a small stream just within ear shot. Sappho calmed the man down and I heard her asking him tender questions. I kept my distance and forced a stoical attitude pro temp.

"Theo, this man is distraught, his wife is dying, says he can't bear the sight of her anymore, he's inconsolable!"

The old man stood upright. He was dressed with quality, openly wearing his excellent sartorial gift. His eye sockets sunken in - black pits, scorched shell holes. His hair was a mess of grey, black and white tumbleweed.

Sappho, "Come on sir we'll take you home, is it far?"

Just behind him I saw a suffering aged gate half open, the three of us struggled with its obstinacy and pushed our way through into a wonderful organised world of garden. A crazy paved path led us to a door and we entered a lovely home. The man waved us to follow him upstairs. A lovely smell of wax polish permeated the musky ambiance of exemplary wooden furniture. No dust settled here.

Sappho and I entered a bedroom. The crying stranger pointed to a huge unkempt bed, his laboured breathing from climbing the staircase gave way to a wail of remorseful sorrowful sounds he pointed to a rolled up section of bedclothes.

"Help her!" he shouted, appearing to gain control, "please don't let her die!"

Sappho reached over to the centre of the bed and carefully turned back a sheet and blanket. Our eyes met. I walked toward the revealed upper body of the deceased.

"Cold and rigor!" whispered Sappho.

The old woman was clothed in a wedding dress. Following a brief acknowledgement of the demise of the young lady, we turned to console her husband.

To our urgent surprise he had disappeared. We searched the home and garden and finally agreed to exit via the rickety gate through which our elderly host had led us through. We struggled and pushed the gate. A vision of an airfield greeted us. Gone where the young trees, bushes and bracken. Sappho and I looked at each other absolutely dumbfounded. I heard an engine struggle and splutter, Sappho pointed across a field of mature wheat.

"Theo! Over there".......

I stared toward the place she was pointing....

A yellow DH Tiger Moth bounced a couple of times - inches from the tarmac and with ease was airborne.

Choices

I would rather walk alone in darkness,

Than in the company of a deceiver.

I would rather shake hands with the devil,

Than look into the eyes of a disingenuous man.

Give me a friend, a strong perceiver.

One who is blessed with a fire fuelled by honest passion;

And I will crawl in confidence,

Through ragged lands,

And drink from a simple nest,

His scarred and bloodied hands.

Hands Off

These special people will look at you, and go. If you are lucky you will see one of these individuals again, you will not be able to thank or love them. All that is important on these chance meetings is eye contact.

This can be so intense it can feel uncomfortable, too intimate to be polite. This is a particular person who has recently helped you. It is an exceptional circumstance. Your problem may have been superficial and long forgotten. Without the special persons intervention we have assumed that things could have had a more serious outcome.

The eye contact is similar to the eye –lust intensity during sex. In our experience it is futile to try and investigate and identify this person. They appear to be folk who walk between two existences, an angelic materialisation if you wish.

In most cases there is a common desire to track down the giver of the look, we record that all attempts have been unsuccessful. This includes CCTV etc. Quite a few-what we call *gifted and aware* contacts accept the sighting and move on. Most note that once the look is over, following the intensity of meeting of two sets of eyes, they experience a sort of ethereal warm loving sensation, albeit this is brief.

The event has meaning. It should not be shrugged off but acknowledged and remembered. The "look" is not coincidental, one cannot seek it. In contrast, the look from a stranger is soon forgotten. You will realise the difference, the look from a helper will engrave itself onto your soul; once experienced it will linger in the mind for days until it is accepted as a great phenomenon.

A genuine contact experience will be recalled for the duration of life as it will be emotionally imbedded.

All of our recorded meetings thus far have been made in a public places. The look is recorded as a sudden desire to react to an invisible force-which pulls our vision into the eyes of a well-wisher.

We have documented that well-balanced genre of sightings occur-no bias. There are no great age gaps, however we have no record of a child bringing reassurance; we do not know why this is. The giver of the look is predominately a post adolescent to mature person.

And so you have it, which is what our little society is all about, La Vista, bringing folk together who have experienced this wonderful glimpse of split second mutual understanding.

Thank you for kicking things off on social media. We are in our infancy but growing day by day. We can demonstrate and confirm that the look is not just something in our imagination. There are a group of caring people out there helping us to get through tough times, decisions and consequences of our actions. Just to re affirm, tracing has proved impossible.

Ok, obviously you have my contact details, maybe one day we could meet up…….

"We have? And when was that…….?

A cold day

Retired; nothing to do; exhaustive morning the afternoon to face, maybe I should remember you. I switch off everything I felt was required.

November is dripping with grey paint and life is thin with undercoat.

My overcoat swings loose in the damp gloomy sway of last day in the month. I don't think I will visit again after today's sojourn.

In this garden, time is spent too much. There are quite a few paying. Paying their respects; paying, paying their respects, respects, it is burning money. Hard earned life is squandered here. The car shivers in the parking bay. I carry a poor excuse for a bunch of petrol station flowers.

Hours and minutes Lowry between headstones and teddy bears heads. I look around and the colour grey greets me, quickly followed by brown, golden brown, those autumn leaves from the songs.

More folk brush by praying their respects. The crematorium is nothing but a one act stage.

I paid not so long ago to scatter the combined ashes of my parents. The operative gently mixed the remains together. I chose the battleship coordinates for the sprinkling operation and off we went.

It was coffee grinder and the occupying human beans put up no resistance even to the wind, and job done.

I recited the ashes to ashes mantra.

Shivered.

And now a return to see if my heart has softened to sentiment as I feel it should. I could have stayed in the warmth of the living room but I was bored and wanted to exorcize this haunting like all sincere pious people do.

Following in the traditions of pile them high sell them cheap (when they're gone they're gone) I cheapen the maudlin me, see - we are all trapped in parenthesis.

What I want to see

Funeral

In;

Nobody's fault but mine   Ry Cooder (Prodigal Son Album)

Midway:

Pyramid Song   Radiohead

Out;

Who will take my dreams away   Angelo Badalamenti & Marianne Faithfull

Note:

Regarding the above request, music is to take precedent over eulogy and formalities.

Flashes;

I witnessed my grandmother rolling pastry with a beer bottle. Her aged long haired Collie dog "Owen" sat, as always, under her scruffy kitchen table. Owen was dressed in long knotted black and grey. Nan and grandads rear garden was very overgrown with the front smaller garden being a First World War trench top of barbed rose branches. The smell of wet dog and lamb fat greeted anyone who stood at the open front door. A canary wouldn't have survived.

The two old parents had raised four children (three girls and a boy) in a town centre terrace, Early 1930's. They moved to a more modern mid 50's home and hosted their offspring and at that time, a single grandchild for occasional Sunday dinners.

I was too young to know that this scene was one of poverty. I cannot remember anyone trying to tidy up the gardens, or scrub the kitchen table.

The family described above was my Mother's side, my Father's, looking back where slightly more organised-four children, three boys and a girl. Their privet edge was trimmed often, lawns cut, dog exercised and there was always a rich smell of furniture polish. I cannot remember ever eating around a table there.

One Christmas under my *poor* grandparents table, I looked and nanny's slippers, there was a huge hole in the sole of one - newspaper could be seen. Now I think how "together" Nan and grandad were in their age. Just like poor slippers, once one is worn out the pair is useless. So it was to be. They spent the last few months together in a tiny OAP's bungalow, grandad lost one leg, then the other, nan diminished, Owen went "missing" I say this in inverted comma's because they just couldn't manage looking after the collie, the collie, in its struggling years, never strayed (went missing)?

As I grew (fighting it all the way) into a teenager my mind questioned a lot of stuff. I rarely visited my grandparents. Not because I had no feeling, but listening to my parents, it seemed so soul destroying, such an exhausting end game that to be frank I didn't want to witness it. The mid to late sixties saw both sets of grandparents packing. Not one made it into their seventies. Needless to say that there were no squabbles over possessions or property; a few quid here, a couple of hundred there.

My parents battled on a lot longer, my Mother escaping dementia at 89, my father sleep walked into 90 years old. As an only child, I picked up the detritus, helped a few charities; assisted three grandchildren with a percentage of overall inheritance.

My wife has also experienced the wet blanket that is the result of the death of ones parents. Her father was killed in a hit and run drink driving incident at 52 years, my mother in law was also given a dementia ticket out of this word at 83 years.

At work the aforementioned actors on Shakespeare's stage toiled as Foundry men, miners, mechanics, bakers, millenary and shop assistants. Each one hard working and loyal, some earned respect by fighting in a war, or serving National Service.

None of the aforementioned walked the way according to worship. Most tolerated hymns and carols when required.

Dec 2020:

Feeling shattered, saturated and marinated in this hell of a human condition.

Picking a book up, tossing it to one side-placing a cd into the JVC, typing and never listening to the music. I don't hear a note. I am disinterested in what the lyrics say; just hoping above anything else the anxiety goes away and into the laptop scream.

Covid and subsequent variant December 19th. This announcement as I type this brings another level of depression and the question-what is the triumph of life? We can blow away 100,000 Japanese lives with one pear drop. We cannot foresee, are blind and through greed we become fat brained and ugly.

I run like some dirty Dickensian tramp and pick up another bottle of Polish 9%.

This will aid the decent into semi oblivion ready for bed; wake up dead, dumbing down the intellect- alcohol fed.

Plagiarism, I lay down my weary head, Shelley! **There will never fucking be A Triumph of Life! Sorry mate!**

Worrying about the continuation of life on our planet is shear folly. This blue ball will be traveling through space laughing all the way, laughing in the face of the human race, time; a Nano second shall we fart and depart. End of.

In this brief story I have omitted love. The passion if you can detect any is only brought on by alcohol, not some omnipotent impotent God; but a chemical reaction to natural attraction and last but not least, a fine mix of sugars and yeast.

We are as useless as a sponge cake left out in the rain.

In the sixties my parents were steaming ahead and due to my father driving with the handbrake on financially things got heated. It accumulated when I was testosterone prone and asked, "Dad, can we have another candle on please?"

I was given a mortgage book with £12 quid in it. I was an apprentice draughtsman in Walsall, my parents mortgage agent lived next door to our office. It was 1970. Dad said, "Take this payment in, and take bloody care of it, it's the final one!

I was aged five when we moved from a terraced house in Lord Street-Walsall, to a posh province-Aldridge in 1957. My parents, where joyful, house paid off in half the time, book stamped, final zero balance and statement. Things at home continued to be tense however. At the end of my mother, dad had paid out circa £85,000 + as mother had to be self-funded in care home for 8 years. Sacrifice over, Dad took just 18 months after her demise to pack up and go to a place without ice and snow.

He was a smart engineer in a foundry, but a mean bastard. I remember vividly one argument when I had loaned a friend an LP, it was returned scratched and scuffed.

"How many bloody times have I told you?"

"Never-Ever trust anyone, it doesn't matter if its God almighty, never trust anyone!"

"You're a Pratt!"

This was a bee sting.

Just memories now; memories. In relation to how things are in 2020, most of the previous writing is just distraction. We have computers, ancestors had wars. Physical conflicts with named antagonists; today the word "cyber" is commonly used. Poison on door handles, clean thefts from accounts and institutions reign ok.

So instantly this story is aimed at my successors, ok, you can read it babe, "its old stuff we know what you went through!"

But we were warned. 3 great novels, We, Brave New World, 1984.

Whatever the human can imagine, sooner or later it will be done. In the end as I say the nice blue planet without humans will wend its way.

But before then, my own demise. Just lost a drinking friend, who had been ill for several months, he gradually his away until I got the news that he left us on Christmas day. It kinda focuses down onto oneself. He gently withdrew from the scene during Covid. Pubs were either shut or under special Perspex and complex track and no face. He hated this. Our drinking pal walked away, enquiries brushed away; all was away…so we gave up. I called at his tiny "Gods waiting room" bungalow, offered food (as he did for my wife and I when we were ill) With each call the door was slower to answer, until one day a stranger opened the door and reported that he was in a deep sleep. Another visit, he's in hospital, several weeks passed then a phone call. Gone. Non Covid (64yrs).

Stuff that we talked about whilst drinking were at best lewd in content, sometimes tails of past mistakes and regret, food, music, and a whole spectrum. The conversation I knew to be exaggerated, riddled with untruth and questionable facts.

So I am thinking. Thinking at 68.

That I remain sexually pass-offable.

That I can still knock the booze back.

That I retain an up to date dress sense.

That I am free from debt.

That I can handle fast cars.

That I have my own teeth.

That I can still write, draw, make and fly radio control aircraft,

That I can still eat Bangalore Phall curries.

That I can still master technology.

That I can hold a good conversation about almost anything (except fucking sport).

That I can still orgasm underwater without bursting for air.

This is esoterically what remains inside. Exoterically I paint tired old man who nobody listens too.

I already knew what kind of people my parents were, I was within their circle most of their lives. When I cleared the house following my father's death I didn't spend too much time sitting on the edge of their double bed looking at photos. If I survive my wife, it would be nice to engage a neutral party to tidy up, or Moth ball. Because all that I have left behind is the product of two individuals who tried their best; my wife's craft skills and her husband's reading and writing efforts. In short our disappearing footprints on the face of this earth will only depress those that follow; and conclude that life is after all absolutely fucking pointless.

Indoor coal fire analogy. Don't overload early flames with the weight of coal, coal has potential but is a late starter. Paper roars with encouragement, kindling wood gives urgent energy and shouldn't be stifled. This is the character of fire and life. Make peace with each other and share the triumph of warmth and happiness.

Second large Lockdown

Just a few days in, been here before; It isn't pleasant.

Morning, breakfast in bed, shower, wash dishes, prepare tea/supper previously agreed upon. Clean out and prepare open fire. Check temperature adjust to suit pocket. (Staying at home is proving more expensive). Make bed, organise laundry, choose the same outer clothes as any other day. I vacuum all around the house with as much interest as a last day at work. It is frosty again; this winter seems to be dragging on in a revengeful icy darkness. The TV news is vomiting negativity.

I step into the back garden. I glance around at our 35 years of fidgety involvement. There is perished herbal patch, a lawn, grapevines, a couple of fruit trees, holly, ivy, rockery, pond, birdbath, shed and greenhouse; all very busy indeed in its meagre 40 x 25 feet. Within the width of 25 feet is a gate. Each side of the gate there are 5ft x 6ft panels, behind these (accept the gate area) is a solid 7ft high Hawthorne bush. This runs spasmodically down a canal tow path.

I have taken a drink of Silent Pool. I stand at a crossroads. My past is behind me. There's a guardian at my right and left hand, one is staring skyward, and the other looks at the earth. Before me a path remains and I step forward.

I open the locks on the gate. I look in each direction at the canal as it diminishes into where and there. The wildlife is hungry. There are no humans to spoil the prospect.

I am greeted by all the mysteries of the black abys of canal, still and flirtatious, it would only take a few minutes to devour me. A young girl 43 years married - with three children is sitting on a settee behind me in a semi warm lounge. She is totally unaware of my contemplations. Every action has consequences.

I have thought this through.

Deeply.

Brownhills

Hardly had the light of day been filed

And entered into the eyes a fresh born child,

We pause for some words from a deity - none.

No action can be taken,

No deeds will bring him back,

He's gone.

He was that little ray of light we look for when the world is black.

He has touched the hearts of many folk,

Given each and every one a kiss in turn,

A reminder a buried minor of hope and eternal bliss,

The tot has already learned to walk there,

In a better place than this.

Fading

I don't think. It's automatic. My mind seems to have given up. I ache. My heart beats whenever it wants. My temper cuts in out of the blue. I have lightening sharp pains in my brain. My left hand, the chord hand sometimes cramps up and fingers twist. Most annoying, the memory is shot. I used to blame my habit of overthinking and trying to do more than one actions at the same time. Now things are scary for me as I am anticipating stuff that may affect my ability to reason. I am sticking with this situation though. It is the year of covid19 and 9 months in. I know how difficult it is to secure a doctor's appointment. I have walked through our district hospital many times since March 29th 2020. I understand the situation.

It seems to me as if my body is really too tired to continue supporting my life.

It is like this.

Things I used to enjoy seem to be out of reach. My reputation for sartorial detail has fled. I wear what is easiest to reach in the wardrobe. My taste and vigour for preparing food has vanished. I snack and pretend it's enough. I shower, and sloppy shave. I gaze from pock marked glass at the world moving from dawn to dusk. I can recall all my career and family life as some frenetic fast forward/rewind. My childhood memories are slow and lamenting. I am frightened and scared of being alone now.

I am frightened and terrified of being alone now.

Through the pock marked dusty windows I see a society that has changed. Everywhere there is an individualist selfishness. I sense this. Expressions are suppressed. Emotions swing easily from alarmist to platonic at best.

The best way I can describe the position I'm in is this.

All my efforts to be a child to person to old man are represented by playing cards. The present is falling backward. There are no more playing cards today. Dawn will bring the same vision as the day before now. From hence forth there is this great slowing down and a very disinterested person in a ragged skin. The daily life is the witnessing of cards falling down. The parenthesis is no more, I am no more. There is a great anxiety with bouts of calm. This will balance out eventually to ultimate annihilation of me; a wiping of the blackboard to facilitate the education of those that will follow this misery.

The situation, when one comes to terms with it, can be very calming. A book produced, a tale well written, the author knows when to end it, not to dwell.

Retirement from work means the shade of grey is bursting with white skin hanging ugliness, a human spent.

Calling

I'm calling for you from a tiny place down here on your black carpet.

I'm calling now because I know your intensions.

I'm calling out.

Don't forget I am here.

I'm aware of your plans.

I'm calling to you.

Silence.

You have chosen not to respond.

I shall not call out to you again.

Goodbye.

Don't cry.

You will find me.

When it's too late and,

All of your plans and intensions have fallen from your hands downward,

Onto the black carpet.

FFS

Nobody can do it for you.

You have to do it yourself.

If you think someone will come and do it for you,

You'll be left on the shelf.

Even if it's changing a tyre,

Folk respect a trier.

Or making a right or wrong decision,

That you learn from, you can walk tall proud and erect!

Work hard, do it, gain self-respect.

If you are frightened of failure,

You're not alone.

Everyone gathered around you,

Have feared mockery and ridicule.

Do it! so all around can witness,

You're a trier and not a lazy fool.

NUT

In the library of my mind,

All book spines are facing in.

In the library of my mind,

Spines are thick to thin.

I am the only one present,

In this empty cell.

I had a lot to say

But nothing to tell.

Now the dust gathers,

In the Library of my mind.

I remain the only one gathered,

I will light the fucking match,

And let the folk who follow,

Start from fucking scratch.

When days don't need no Names

Song for guitar

When days don't need no names,

And distance becomes too much

I will not question what *he* proclaims,

When I'm anxious for your touch.

When the Sun and Moon reflect no light,

From your Sun so far away,

And night becomes my comfort cloth,

To *him*, I'll turn and say,

When all five senses fail me, Lord,

And the days no longer have names,

Take me away to that happy place,

But, let me see her happy face,

On that day that had no name.

Only Feelings please,
I have no name.

I am lost cold-hungry and depressed.

I cannot be bothered to stand and get dressed.

There must be someone behind me,

A queue; a thin lost soul.

Don't just stand behind me!

Make yourself known.

Please come and find me

Please come,

Find me.

Take me fucking home.

The Dawning of Old Age

The fishing forecast usually wakes me up. It's enough to give you the pip; I shudder imagining I'm on that ship.

Swish back the curtains to view a copper dusk. I struggle to dress as my trousers shit a sock. Look down at the midriff but look back up just as fast, the hole and the button have announced their engagement at last.

My face is a blind window cleaner's leather, hard to tell what's holding it together.

I have walnut arms, legs, hands and feet; an ancient bog man dug up from peat.

From some way off I smell a familiar fire. The toaster reminds me I'm due to expire.

I stagger past a full length and see triple knees, another sock lodged? They don't come in three's.

Today I cannot see the point.

It will end once again, a reversal of the above, as common as a beef joint.

The same repugnance I feel toward sprouts; they are farts dressed up as septic spouts. The carpet as usual is out to get me, my jumper snags on a handle, as I carry a hot mug of tea.

So now it looks like I have pissed myself. There will be a knock on the door later, and the girl I love-my attendee, (god how I hate her) will fuss, reprimand and make light of it all. The front door will close and that will be that; another day ended a tea stained crutch, a sinking feeling, a kind of dizzy reeling, and back to bed.

I miss the company of a silk skinned woman so much. I'm as anxious as the day I was born, but no longer have nipples and smiles to keep me warm.

The fishing forecast usually sends me to sleep. If only I could pull the rope from the keep.

The Messy Poet

She knows that by wearing certain apparel,

I'll have her in my sights.

Looking down the length of my barrel,

Each chance meeting, every date becomes a battle;

A confusion of black cattle in the night.

I am a fox insane with delight,

She seductively

Provokes me

With her certain apparel.

I have her in my sights,

We wrestle in private darkness

I fire.

I fire several times.

I die.

She rolls away into a hell of hot pitch,

Into the cold steaming cattle of a black night.

I lose her again, and once more, again and again.

My poetry is as common as her milk.

Shock and Oar

If I should turn to go,
And not say Cheerio!
Think only this of me.

Wanker!

The Walker

She rejoices in her independent infertility,

She is a maypole for her flock of dogs,

A flock of dogs, a flock of dogs,

She's obedient to the holy trinity;

She walks under a cool dripping sky,

With her flock of dogs, flock of dogs,

Shale and sea and trees,

They tug and flurry,

Around her knees,

The flock of dogs, the flock of dogs,

Under the grey sky devoid of gods,

She walks her flock of dogs,

Her flock of dogs.

Plates, knives and forks

When your family and mates transform into spinning plates,

It's time for self-preservation.

Let the plates fall.

They're all self-centred,

Pre occupied with their selves.

Stand back now and watch the show,

Without your pious contribution,

They will thrive briefly in your wishes; and fail.

Like hail and snow they will diminish and rest.

Leave you questioning,

Was I true to my family, a friend, or pest?

Beware of the last spinning plate!

This is without a doubt the person you most hate.

Printed in Great Britain
by Amazon